Children of the Rose

Children of the Rose

ELAINE FEINSTEIN

HUTCHINSON OF LONDON

HUTCHINSON & CO (Publishers) LTD
3 Fitzroy Square, London W1

London Melbourne Sydney Auckland
Wellington Johannesburg Cape Town
and agencies throughout the world

First published 1975
© Elaine Feinstein 1975

Set in Intertype Baskerville

Printed in Great Britain by The Anchor Press Ltd
and bound by Wm Brendon & Son Ltd
both of Tiptree, Essex

ISBN 0 09 123150 7

For Arnold

I

The château of Alex Mendez was cut into sedimentary white rock above a small Provençal village, south-east of Avignon. The village had been deserted by its local population sometime during the nineteeth century, and apart from a few houses round the old market-place, most of the small buildings had fallen into ruin beyond repair. Above the towers of the château itself rose a skeleton ridge of eroded stone, with nothing more than a little bramble and brushwood in the gorges; and the stones of the building itself had been collected from the same brutal landscape. Its severe structure made harsh corners of black shadow against the sun. Below the terrace olive trees, a few vines, wild asparagus, and a field of aromatic lavender led downhill towards massive iron gates.

The whole area had a murderous history. Mendez' lawyer Tobias Ansel judiciously set this out among his reasons for discouraging the purchase. In the gardens, where slabs of rock lay about like half-excavated relics, a dried-up well-shaft had been the site of several notorious acts of savagery. Smaller in scale, certainly, than those of Languedoc, where all the lepers were burnt in 1321; and not to compare with the great massacres of the Jews at Narbonne and Carcassonne; nevertheless the local stories had an uneasy resonance. At the time of the plague a group of flagellants, exiled from the local church, had set up the formal circle of their rite around the well; in their frenzy, a few yellow-toqued strangers, whom they intended to baptize by force, had fallen under the leather thongs of their scourges. Later, a papal emissary of rebuke from Avignon had been torn apart by a mob of wild penitents at the order of their Master.

Mendez shrugged the stories away: All Europe tastes of blood, he said.

—Considered as an investment, began Tobias Ansel, kicking at a line of giant ants filing out of a crevice in the rock wall.

—Oh, absolutely a folly, agreed Mendez.

—Exactly. You admit it.

—I know it, said Mendez, amused : So?

—And Lalka?

—My fair-haired English Tobias, Mendez replied patiently : Look at these stony *garrigues*. Who is there to please here? Would I be less conspicuous in Saint Tropez, do you think? Or England perhaps? Some wooded acres in the south-west? Tell me, where was it your Flemish ancestors buried their skill in cutting gems, so you could go to Winchester and Oxford?

Mendez stood with his legs apart and hands on his hips, a light blue T-shirt sticking to his neck, and to shoulders that were still thick and powerful. His forehead rose across his shiny freckled scalp in a long oval; his only remaining hair was a brown frizz above each ear. It was a coarse, handsome face, even a tough face, until he took off his sunglasses; and then his brown eyes looked unexpectedly large and melancholy.

But he smiled. He understood so exactly the faint involuntary dilation of Ansel's nostrils as he spoke of Lalka. She embarrassed Tobias. He flinched in her presence. When they met, he did not know how to parry her embraces. Everytime he was drawn into her musky hair and against her exposed white flesh; poor Tobias, who hated to touch and be touched. Lalka must have known as much. It must have pleased her to violate him.

—I think she will prefer to stay in Cheyne Walk, said Alex rather sadly. And could at once see Lalka against the green velvet of her button-backed chair. Why should she want to move? Now? A fine, bold woman, Mendez reflected. Who had once been his wife. A little shrewd about the mouth, perhaps; with her black eyes on the fine print of the last settlement.

Her room smelled of fresh lemons on their last visit, he remembered. And Tobias had still walked about it with some tension widening his nose. Mendez knew why. It was more than the aroma of middle-aged sexuality that alarmed him. It was Poland; it was that landscape of the dead Tobias scented. So many of them. In mineshafts and tunnels, gulping for air in the sludge; in stale rainwater, mixed with clay, shivering; in ash and potash; lime-kilns; rags in the mud. In fishmeal, behind fences, in freight-cars. Horrors for which Tobias felt nothing but disgust.

They were not his inheritance. Every feature declared as much. His hair, eyebrows and eyelashes were almost pale enough to suggest a genetic defect in pigmentation; his eyes were a deep northern blue. He wore his hair combed flat to his head; and his pallor was accentuated by unfashionably dark clothing. His face also was unusually thin, with a particularly long chin, which gave him a fleeting resemblance to Fred Astaire. But his eyes glittered with something closer to malevolence than gaiety.

—And what about the rest of them? *They* might like a change.

Lalka was childless. Mendez knew Ansel was thinking now of his poor sister-in-law Clara, and her husband Peretz.

—Is it likely? Alex put aside a little guilt at the thought. Snapshots of Clara as a young girl fell through his mind;

9

laughing against sand-dune and lake; hugging her sons; an innocent beauty. And then he settled comfortably on the image of the short, red-cheeked drudge Clara had become; her breasts and belly hanging downward in one continuous sagging slide. Peretz was a brute.

—I am not planning a family rest-home, he said firmly.

—But you will live here?

—Three or four months of the year.

—While I stay in Antwerp?

—I shall need you there, said Mendez quietly.

Tobias shrugged: And if I prefer London?

—Now don't be offended. I understand your anxiety, Tobias. You want me, of course, to live modestly. But the trouble is I am too old for it. And in any case it is no protection for a Mendez. Believe me. In England nobody understands that.

—Because it isn't true.

—On that point we won't quarrel. Tell me, Mendez asked: what happened to the fourth tower? Over there. He pointed. Tobias smiled: I was coming to that. Sometime in the eighteenth century an explosion destroyed it. Some student of Arab hermetic philosophy, I believe, was engaged in the transmutation of perfect matter at the time.

Mendez laughed until his shoulders shook gently: Are you afraid I may take up his example?

—I don't know what you're up to. Whatever it is, the building is too big, said Tobias, irritably: Some of the rooms are open to the belfry. You will go mad here. And why do you want to disappear? In any case. You are not yet fifty.

—I shall work on my own a while, said Mendez: Think. Read a little history.

—In that case you will go mad.

Mendez laughed.

—In this region, said Ansel: they use the word *fada*. For men who want to see what no one else can.

—Do you think I am looking for God?

—You obstinate old man, said Ansel: You don't even know. But you will be a local scandal, all the same, and soon enough.

—In this desert?

—Every pretty girl on the coast will home in on you like a bat, said Ansel gravely.

—Really? Well. They sound safe enough. In any case, you are my lawyer, said Mendez: Not my guardian. Buy this monster. If there is anyone still alive to sell it. What else should I do? From now on? Lay my bones at the foot of Sainte Victoire with the other dinosaurs? I am not quite ready for the cemetery.

There were things Alex did not choose to explain. It was thirty years ago, and not too far from this eroded hillside, in the house of an old friend, that Alex had patiently waited for his own father to die, with two airline tickets in his pocket. Guiltily hidden. At seventy, Mendez' father had lain propped against six pillows like a tree stump, his distended legs thrust out ahead of him. His eyes were veined and yellow, and his face was cracked like parched mud. Bushes of white hair met over his nose and hung over his eyes, and a few long strands continued to grow out of his nostrils. He lay very still; but evidently his thoughts went on turning, like the swallows dipping again and again in vineyards below his window. He had come south in March, with Alex, and now it was late July. The soil was already white powder; the grass like straw; the week before a whole hillside had broken into flame.

The local cook continued to make dishes with black olives and the heavy, sweetish oil his father had once loved; she baked bread for him in the enormous ovens; and tempted him with thrush pâté. Before his illness the old man had eaten gluttonously, and drunk a litre of wine a day. Now he could do neither of those things; but it pleased him to have the food prepared. He ate soft fruit which two nurses pared for him; sometimes he complained that his false teeth tasted like iron. They were pretty, willing girls; no doubt off-duty they looked like birds of paradise. At the bedside they sat solemnly and decorously and tended his father's fifteen stones of torpor without chattering. As far as Alex could judge, he must have felt little pain. When he did, one of the nurses gave him an injection. Sometimes he called out in a language they did not speak, and they did not listen.

Alex slept, while the morphine made his father's mind wander. Outside the wells dried, the grasshoppers sang; but his father was walking through village streets that smelled of milk and horses; a spoilt child of scrawny aunts, conjurors, tailor uncles. Surrounded with the aroma of honey and cinammon and all the tastes of his childhood; sweet herrings and poppyseed bread. And his bedside thronged with visitors. They kept a constant vigil with him through his dreams. In moments of insomnia, Alex also felt their eyes upon him; waiting for him. Towards the end, afloat in his bed, his father began to pass through the landscape of the dead, as if *he* were a visiting ghost, and *their* presence the solid reality. In this way, he passed fitfully for whole nights through a flat land drained by old-fashioned cuts, where the sun fell obliquely through white rain.

Always, between sleep and waking, he was haunted by whatever shone in the dark. Small fish, phosphorescent lichen, pink quartz. Sparks from the eyes of invisible animals. As if some subtle fire rose continuously about him.

Some of this, at least, he described to his son.

After lunch, Alex usually took Pastis with the doctor on the terrace, and sometimes they played chess. Their conversations usually went coldly; Alex felt himself disliked. On the day of his father's death the newspapers were particularly ominous and the weather made everyone uneasy. Over the chessboard, Alex took refuge in perversity. He moved his bishop, slyly, speculatively, and took another sip of the cloudy aromatic liquid; then he murmured : Have you ever thought about diamonds?

The doctor stared down at the board, with a sour expression intended to express both his distaste for the boy's accent, and a resentment at his oblique manner. Certainly he was an awkward child; no offer of sympathy was ever possible. At the moment, in any case, his interests seemed wholly antiquarian.

—I understand diamonds were prescribed once, Alex said : by members of your profession. For those suffering from fevers. And to expel poisons.

—No doubt, said the doctor, uneasily shifting in his wicker chair, with a hand uncertainly on his remaining knight.

—The etymology of the word is also interesting, said Alex : Have you ever read Albert? He wrote about minerals in the thirteenth century. I think they canonized him in 1931. According to Albert, the diamond is the stone of a *daimon*; of course, that could mean either a good or an evil spirit. As the stone is called the bow of the daimon because it has two colours.

The wind was rising. Clouds of white dust rose between the dead straw and began to blow across their feet. Alex sneezed. The sun was like a hard yellow stone in the sky. The man and the boy were sitting in the shade of two trees with fat trunks, mottled as if with disease. Between them, a hammock began to creak as the wind caught the

13

upper branches. Alex was to remember that noise, and saying: This climate gives me a headache. He even remembered the doctor's brief grunt of superiority. Then there was a cry from one of the upper windows.

His father had been trying to get out of bed. In spite of his illness and the slowness of his movements, his weight and determination made it difficult for the two nurses to prevent him. Whatever he saw at that moment, it was something he was determined to catch; if necessary by throwing his whole bulk across it.

As Alex and the doctor arrived in the doorway, Mendez was on all fours; an awkward and ferocious animal, panting over a coloured scarf, which he was trying to grasp in dry, enervated fingers.

A little white patch gleamed on the wooden floor.

—I'll give him a sedative, said the doctor, not moving, however, towards the gross and still formidable figure. The nurses too had drawn back. But in some way a sense of some new and surrounding presence had reached the sick man. The great head raised, but uncertainly, and unfocussed eyes travelled around the room. He seemed to pinch all the muscles of his face together, screwing up his nose and eyes in one huge effort of concentration.

—Alex, he said. And then looked down in bewilderment at the green chiffon he had bunched in his hands.

Once safely back in bed, the old man asked for his son; and when Alex sat beside him he took one slim young hand between his own, on which the skin was now dry as paper. His eyes were shining, as if he were still in the grip of some revelation of loveliness. Alex found it too hard to catch his words; there was something about the stars of the sky entering the room, something about

Alex' mother. Alex felt in his pocket for clean linen to wipe his father's head, and felt instead the Moroccan wallet, the passport, the hidden tickets. Then suddenly his father's lips parted in a smile. He pressed his son's hand with his remaining strength. Now he would surely speak. But the voice remained largely inaudible. In every great breath there were so many consonants. And Alex sat by his side to the end. Wooden. Incredulous. *Had* his father really said: God is good? It was late August 1939. The wind was blowing the last dry earth away. At the time Alex had not even understood why it was so important to him to have heard clearly.

The owner of the château in 1970 turned out to be far removed from Provence. His name was Oliver Walsh; and he lived in a flat in Notting Hill, which had a rather fine Georgian frontage and a rubble of plaster and paving stones running down to the slope to his basement. He opened the door himself in a striped and torn dressing gown, short enough to give Ansel a clear view of small purplish balls, and with a bustle of courtesy he led Ansel at once to a room upstairs. As Ansel knew the château had been on the market for about five years, he had not expected Oliver to be putting much energy in trying to promote a sale. He therefore took the man's jumpy eagerness for his habitual manner. Walsh had a narrow, nervy face, which was almost re-shaped by a great frizzy spade of a beard. The only feature which gave a clue to his expression was his mouth, which was a surprising red orifice at the centre of the curling ginger hair. This opening distended into a smile punctually on the last word of each phrase, as if both to clinch his own certainty in what he said, and impose it upon his listener.

—Yes, my mother's, he said at once, with the red smile

much in evidence: She was French, I'm afraid. All her family live down there, but *they've* never taken any interest in the bloody place, of course. *Do* have a drink.

A bottle of surprisingly good red wine stood on a wooden box between two open tins of cat-food.

—The trouble *is*, Oliver continued, with another explanatory grimace: lots of people see it would make a *lovely* hotel, if only they had the money. But nobody has the money these days. So there it sits. Do you like the wine? It *is* good, isn't it? Do you live in London? My wine merchant imports it specially for me, but I can sometimes arrange for friends to get a bottle or two. What do you think of my mirrors?

Ansel observed they were very fine.

—A little man round the corner. If you're interested. Now I wonder if you'd mind coming up another flight of stairs with me? Then I'll change, and after that I suppose I'd better run you quickly round to the office.

He sighed, as if at the waste of time: But first do tell me what you think of the bedroom. I think it's going to be a *very* successful piece when it's finished.

Certainly the room was far more advanced in décor than any other part of the house. It was carpeted in purple, and walled in raised lilac paper; a French rococo dressing table jostled a huge velvet-backed double bed. Tobias looked around desperately for something to praise; and then noticed what looked like a genuine Fragonard hanging on the only free wall.

—From the château? he enquired.

—*Isn't* it lovely? agreed Oliver: I'm so glad you enjoy it.

—The light's always wrong for him in the north, though, isn't it? said Tobias. He was unprepared for the expression of immediate pain produced on Oliver's face by his remark.

16

—*Do* you think so? *Really?*

Oliver paused, without his dressing gown, revealing his full round belly for Ansel's inspection, and studying the picture carefully. It struck Tobias that Oliver was in some way enjoying the exposure of his genitals.

—Perhaps it's brighter here in the mornings? Tobias suggested.

—No, you're *right*, I think, said Oliver. He sounded faintly depressed : But then I never go to France, horrible country. Haven't been back since Mother died.

—I'm sorry, said Ansel.

—No need to be sorry about *that*, said Oliver, pettishly : It was years ago and I hated her anyway. Resistance heroine, they say : or *some* do. I *have* heard nastier stories.

—Did you know her well?

Oliver's thoughts had wandered off among the underwear.

—These? he asked.

—By all means.

—Now *this* place, said Oliver : *this* is an intelligent investment. Rather clever of me to find it, don't you think?

He put on neat black-rimmed spectacles at this point and observed Tobias Ansel's remarkable appearance for the first time in focus. For a moment his eyes looked round and surprised as black buttons.

—I expect you'll be wondering, he said slowly : how I fit in with old Lord Whatsit and the rest of the family?

Ansel had already looked this up, but did not mention it.

—Well, said Oliver, with evident pleasure : not distantly enough, I'm afraid. They all disapproved of my mother, of course. Quite rightly. But now she's gone, they're *all* over me. I *hate* families.

Ansel went over to look out of the window and opened it. What a lovely city, he thought, London was. How many trees, how the rain filled the squares with the taste of leaves and humus; how the scent rose up even into this squalid attic. Yes, he loved England. He would live nowhere else in the world.

Lying on the floor, with a few papers at his feet, lay a photograph in a silver frame, with the glass broken. A thin-lipped, clear face, with fine eyebrows drawn over pale eyes, stared up at him with an ambiguous amused expression; the tender features had just a faint suggestion of viciousness, as those of a caged fox might.

—Who's that? asked Tobias involuntarily, picking up the picture. It was not a rudeness of which he would have been ordinarily capable.

—My sister, said Oliver : But you don't have to bother about her. She doesn't hold a share or anything. Fortunately. She's mad, he said, rummaging in the drawers of the delicate dressing table with some violence : We don't get on, he concluded.

Then a great sadness seemed to come over him as he turned, fully dressed in all his outlandish splendour, to face Ansel : I *do* hope you aren't going to go all solemn and depressed after you've seen my lawyer. Why not come back here? I'm a *very* good cook.

—I'm staying at a hotel, thank you.

—I've been very ill, you know, said Oliver : I don't know why, I don't get to see many people these days. It can be very lonely.

—I'm only acting for a client, said Tobias stiffly : I shan't need, you know. Any bolstering.

At once, the sad smile faded.

—A client? Who? Not *black*, is he? Oliver asked quickly.

—No.

—Pied Noir?

—They aren't, said Ansel, patiently.

—I know *that* my dear man, but one has some responsibilities. Would you have the goodness to tell me : *Who* are you acting for?

With some diffidence Ansel gave Mendez' name.

There was a little silence. Then Oliver Walsh said with perfect composure : Now I hope you do clearly understand that the vineyard *beyond* the wall is not included in the asking price? For the moment.

Sipping a small glass of Armagnac, Alex Mendez watched the fountains of Aix splash together in the amber floodlight; the air about him warm and pine-scented; the Roman statuary outlined against a sky as blue as ink. He sat on his own, at a table with an empty chair, feeling the alcohol rise quietly in his blood. He had spent the day in an uneasy mood; and it had not cleared yet. But certainly he felt better since Ansel had taken the plane for England.

He reflected ungraciously on Ansel's cold eye. Tobias, the necessary angel. How little the man let himself be known; how formally he kept his place and distance. And yet how adequately he conveyed the chill of his disapproval. His purity. Like winter. Of course, his austerity had force and energy in it, almost like a fever. Mendez shrugged. It was a useful sickness. But what, for instance, he speculated, did Tobias do for sex? All speculation foundered on that thought. There was no congress of limbs, either male, female or androgyne, in which Mendez could imagine Tobias' body without a sense of embarrassment.

Across his own consciousness, two voices and the chords of a guitar broke noisily. Two tables away, a black-haired boy of about twenty lay sprawled between his girl-friend's bare legs, playing a folk guitar. Glancing upward from the girl's brown feet, and elegant body, Mendez was a little shocked to read in the pallor of her face and the lines running from nose to mouth that she must be ten years older than her companion. It was a fine face, however; and her voice was remarkable, with a hard peasant stridency that rose over her companion's growl; she drew a little scatter of applause from the middle-aged drinkers at the surrounding tables. As Mendez watched, she threw back her head and laughed; pulling her friend's black hair as she did so, until his head pushed into her crotch so closely that Mendez felt his own flesh stirring at the imagined contact.

Decidedly, Mendez admitted, Tobias' parting gibes had been well founded. Mendez was unredeemably of the flesh. Worse, his present retreat depended on Ansel's alert dedication. With a little shift, Mendez wondered how long it would be before Ansel cut away from him altogether. Shrewdly, he gave himself about two years. Tobias was ambitious, he made no secret of it. But he wasn't ready yet. And whatever he thought of Mendez, irritation would never make him act to his own disadvantage.

Mendez called the waiter again. Perhaps he was celebrating his release from scrutiny a little unwisely? He would have bad dreams again, restless confused dreams; or worse, not sleep at all. Last night he had been annoyed by news from New York which had taken him into the small hours through his spread of investments in a long habit of calculation. He had even found himself phoning Basel, to confirm some mobility he saw developing. Absurd. When it was exactly that waste of life he wanted to draw away from; that had come to seem trivial. Perhaps, after all, it was too late. Perhaps he would never

20

be able to let go the habit of control or be free. Or not nobly free; but always with a hangover of suspicion and watchfulness. In which case his retirement would be false, and fail; all that could come of it would be a gradual sinking into guarded self-indulgence – a faith in wine and whatever could be braised in butter and beer; at last, he would find himself in a vile loneliness, knowing no more than he did now : which was that a splinter of glass or even a fish-bone in the throat could put out thought altogether. A scholar? Now? He should have been bolder at fifteen when his father died. As Tobias had once observed.

Slowly, Mendez put down the new glass of Armagnac in its saucer. The guitar had begun again, and the girl was now singing; an old Piaf song, harsh, assertive and vulgar. But it did not reach him. For some reason, a forgotten dream had come back to him from his disturbed night.

He had been lying as if staked; bound, perhaps, to the four posts of an enormous bed. The red velvet of the curtains was very clear to him; also a long dressing gown chord of red silk, which he knew to be a bell-rope. At the foot of his bed a gold mirror reflected the red velvet drapes and nothing more. With an enormous effort, he had succeeded in bending his neck upward to catch a glimpse of the mirror in an effort to understand his situation. But he could not lift his head into range of the glass. Instead he could see the image of a child, about a year old; held in arms he did not recognize; by someone whose face was in shadow. The child was crying, and holding out her arms. To Mendez, as it seemed. But he was helpless. Slowly the shadowy figure moved away, and the child, too, passed out of his vision. But when he woke, the child's cries had still been in his ears.

Was Tobias in his dream? For a moment

the question seemed strangely important; Mendez scoured his memory, which at once closed as perversely as it had opened. Alex shook his head. And then found himself saying : I beg your pardon?

—*Feu?* Match? It was the girl singer who had come to his table, sidling into the empty chair.

Mendez reached into his pocket for his lighter, and then abruptly changed his mind. The girl's face was bent over her cigarette, and the long brown hair hid her expression; but Mendez was suddenly alerted out of his moody isolation into an absolute certainty that she knew who he was. He picked up the packet of matches on the café table guardedly. He lit her cigarette. He stood up. Tomorrow, he decided, he would move south. Through the Camargue.

2

Afraid. Yes. Since Mendez had left, there were days, bad days; when Lalka paid a taxi and the squint eye of the driver on her velvet coat made her over-tip; when she felt leers of avarice follow her up the quiet street to her house. Especially on late afternoons. When it was dark and wet, and the streets were yellow. In November. Her birthday month. Sometimes she did feel panicky then; like a migrant bird fallen sick.

A bad month to be forty, in any case. In the cold. Sometimes it seemed as if her blood was draining away. And she shook in the wind until her own small hallway closed around her; it seemed so good to shut the pale thick door on the street. Then she could pause before her own mirror, and pat her thick straight hair; let the solidity of her even-featured face reassure her. Look. My eyes are yellow; my skin is still supple; and the bones underneath are tough. Then she would smile, and bend to the letters lying on the ledge beneath.

—Maria, she called now down to the kitchen: any calls for me?

—Hello, Mrs Mendez? Maria's voice came from the flight of stairs above. She was kneeling over a pan and brush; and the face she turned over her great haunches looked a little startled. Lalka saw at once a painted vase had broken: You didn't hear me come in? Well, never mind that now, leave that, she said impatiently: Did you take any messages?

Maria rose heavily to her feet: I think. There was one call. A man.

—Maria, Lalka sighed: how often have I told you? The *name*. Did you write down the name?

—No.

Lalka tapped her teeth with an unopened letter.

—Because it was Mr Tobias. Why write – Mr Tobias? He said he call later. Now I make you a coffee.

Lalka shivered a little: Thank you.

—Also your friend Katie phoned, said Maria, with a certain formality.

Lalka felt a little colour rise into her cheeks.

—I'll call her back.

—She said, any time.

—Yes. Thank you. Lalka bent her face to hide her lips. Because Katie's call was the one she had been wanting. And Maria knew that perfectly well. Damn. The woman had really worked for her too long, she *knew* her. It was intolerable. It was almost as bad as having a man in the house. And yet, what was there to conceal? Lalka felt herself growing confused and restless.

She took off her coat, and sat down by the window facing the river. She was warmer now, but the wet discoloured sky still entered the room; lit the purples in the carpet; and charged the oxblood of her Chinese bowl. Against her will, she could feel unwanted pieces of old conversations begin to leak into her consciousness.

There was Alex' kind, open face.

—Are you lonely? Lalka. You seem depressed.

—Nonsense, she flashed. Too quickly, she had always replied too quickly to Alex: It's just. I can't see how to change. To be what you want, she admitted.

—But you mustn't change! That's a terrible thing to say.
I don't want you ever to try.

—Then how can we go on?

And that was the day she had first seen how it was: that
the question lay between them with its own answer. There
was no need for either of them to go on. And he had
comforted her so strangely: Poor girl, you were never
exactly confident. Of yourself. Never wanting to be what
you could.

—When I married you? Oh, you've forgotten, you've
forgotten. How it was. I never expected. I *never* wanted.

—You refused everything. Why? If only I understood
why.

—Alex, I haven't changed. It's you. I'm the same.

Two voices moving across one another; always at a
slant.

—It's hopeless, Alex said: We are like two monologues.
I give up. Haven't you always, well for a long time,
wanted me to. Leave you alone? And now that I'm off
you look scared.

—Yes.

—What of?

—Ending up some eccentric old woman, she managed
to laugh: Disgusting myself.

—You won't do that, he said quietly: Don't you know?
You'll forgive yourself anything as long as no one is
looking.

And then she had hated him. When had she ever spoken
so cruelly to him?

When had she ever spoken so cruelly to him.

—Even you may find things less idyllic than you think
she said, tonelessly: Who knows? My demands were
small.

—That was my complaint.

—You'll be eaten up.

—I'll experiment.

—There are lots of mistakes. Different every time.

—So you hope.

—Well, yes, in a way I do hope.

—What a bitch you are, he said : Without even knowing it.

Was she a bitch? She couldn't tell. She didn't even understand why Katie had become an issue between them. And yet. To have a woman-friend was new for Lalka. She had never *liked* women; had despised them even; muted, helpless creatures. Always less than their men. Always turned towards them. So Katie was different. She made Lalka feel defiant. Was that so treacherous? To admire someone. Because *that* was the truth of it. She admired Katie because she took risks. She lived rashly.

—Well, you've always played particularly safe, Mendez had agreed ironically.

Lalka hardened, thinking of that. For she had. With reason.

—What reason? If you had children.

Yes, *then* people understood caution. It was respectable. You played safe for them.

—You think me calculating, she said crossly.

—And worse. Because you enjoy your friend's craziness. In your fantasy. Do you think I don't know that?

—You can't taunt me with being *loyal*, Lalka cried.

—How about loyal in the *head*?

—Where?

—In the intent. In your thoughts.

—You think I couldn't have had any man I wanted?

—Of course. But you would have had to take off your clothes, Lalka. You would have had to expose yourself to them. Would you have liked that?

26

—Would *you* have preferred it?

—For me, the thought is the same.

And Alex had hated Katie on sight. The trance-like softness of her short-sighted eyes, her brown presence; the deep voice no longer more than faintly American; the shades of disappointment at the edges of her eyes and lips.

—She's a Lesbian, Alex had insisted.

—Katie? You're joking. With all those husbands?

And it *was* a joke; it was wildly wide of the mark. There was nothing erotic between them. Except, Lalka thought, a certain edgy suspense. This teasing reluctance to phone. As if they were playing a game with one another. She drank the black hot coffee. Opened her letters. One was a card from her sister Clara. Lalka sighed. Poor Clara. Well, she would phone her today.

Instead, of course, she phoned Katie. Who sounded preoccupied. Almost as if she had a book open while Lalka spoke. But at last she said abstractedly: What's happening to you?

—I'm forty, that's how I am, said Lalka.

—Darling, your life should have more interesting dates.

—I can't be bothered, you know? Lalka lit a cigarette: I don't mean the clothes and the hair, I do that anyway, but . . .

—I don't mean days full of *men*, you moron. What you need is a complete change.

—That's right, said Lalka, rather dully.

—A holiday.

—Please, Katie. When I *want* holidays, I have them.

—But I mean a real change. Look, why don't you come away? With me?

Katie worked free-lance for several newspapers.

—Where are you going? asked Lalka, without much excitement. She didn't, after all, need her expenses paid to travel.

—On a job.

—But where?

—East.

—You mean behind the Curtain, East? Lalka swallowed: Well, you know I'm not sure I'd feel too easy about that.

—For Godsake, you've got a British passport, haven't you?

The doorbell went. Lalka shouted down to Maria: Could you get that? Katie, I'll call you, she concluded evasively.

—Think about it.

—I will, Lalka promised.

Then she lit another cigarette, and opened a cabinet of drinks. Without waiting, she poured herself a tall vodka. As she had somehow guessed, her visitor was Tobias Ansel.

She arranged herself for him, out of habit; in response to the step of a man. Slipped off her jacket, threw one arm over the chair-back, tucked up her silky black legs.

—Tobias. How lovely. Her voice rose, provoking him.

And he was looking rather fine in his dark blue suit she thought; clean, like a young Sorel.

—It's my birthday, did you know? she said. And then laughed; because naturally he did. She lit another cigarette, shrugging at his evident disapproval.

—Yes, I smoke too much. And drink.

She threw the end of her last cigarette across the room, into a blue wicker basket filled with papers.

—Too much. Don't worry, she said: The butt was cold.

28

—How are you? he asked.

—Well.

—Are you happy in England?

—I suppose.

Was she? In a flash she doubted that. Thinking of the grey eyebrows and the pink flesh of her friends. And how she no longer existed for the youngsters, sitting round stone fountains, so many of them these days; lying about, unemployed. In the rain. They looked drab and sad. She had passed a group earlier in the day, thinking as much and wondering: what would come of them; as she passed, a roar of laughter had followed her. Surprised, she had turned to gaze at them. In their laughter was no benevolence. They did not see her good looks; only her class and her age. She was comic to them, therefore; and so it must be only among the grey eyebrows and the pink-fleshed that she could live and be welcome. Would that be so everywhere? Perhaps there was more to it. Not just ageing. Not just female anguish. She felt it urgently; again; in the presence of Tobias, in his question. This cold, hard man. Why had Mendez chosen him? Lalka could feel his enmity. *Fear this man.* She wanted to warn Alex. To call a warning. And then she put the thought down. It was only the weather working on her; the strange livid sky getting into her blood.

—How is Alex?

—Fit.

—And the château?

—Expensive, he smiled.

—Will you have some lemon tea? Lalka called: Maria!

—I won't stay long. He paused: Look. I have brought you a present.

—Oh. Lalka was confused: From Alex? Thank you. I will open it. Later.

She took the packet from him with a pang in her throat.

Tobias began to walk about the room. She supposed the heating was up too high. Most men found it so. He looked pale and hemmed in.

—You should travel, he said : Open a window for yourself. On the world.

—Funnily enough, she began. And then stopped. Her distrust of Tobias was profound. She would not even mention Katie's suggestion.

—Maybe you're right. Maybe I need a break. She looked at Tobias shrewdly.

—So. Here you are in London. Cashing up for Alex.

—Not quite. He smiled : It's complicated. We'll do it in our time. That's my job. The timing.

—There's no trouble?

—None. Except the size of it all. It's like dismantling India.

She relaxed for a moment, and laughed with him : You'll enjoy it.

—No, he said quietly : I hall hate it. I think it's grotesque. And irresponsible. It makes no sense to me. Not morally nor politically.

—Or financially?

—Least of all.

—I suppose he wants clean hands, said Lalka softly. Tobias laughed : What a fantasy.

In his eyes she saw he wanted to leave.

—You can't know him, she said breathlessly : you don't understand. His luck. He couldn't avoid it.

—Lalka, he isn't giving anything away, you know.

She took the point. For one moment she let him see her fear : Tobias. Look after him, will you?

Clara's phone stood in the hall by a dusty vase of dried flowers next to a bottle of orange squash. The only light and warmth in the flat were in the kitchen; in the hall-way the lino was broken; and the paintwork was brown. The wind came in a direct line under the felt of the letterbox.

—Who was that? came Peretz' voice.

—Not for you.

—I didn't ask who it was *for*. I asked who it *was*. You were out there long enough.

Clara came back into the harsh light, blinking a little, smiling, running a hand through her hair. She was younger than Lalka, and still looked it; even in her cheap print dress. Her hair was black and curly, and her skin was soft and flower-like.

—Was I? Would you like tea now then? It was my sister.

—Oh, it was.

—Yes.

The man turned from the television and fixed his wife with a pair of deep-set black eyes sunk into a sallow face; unlike his wife, who was plump and red-cheeked, he looked seedy. His face was set in an expression of desperate patience.

—Have you no shame? To mention her? That whore. I won't have you naming her in this house.

—She's not, said Clara quietly.

—And how did your Mendez make his money, if you're so clever? Your marvellous brother-in-law. Tell me that?

—Lalka says, began Clara, foolishly.

—What does *she* know? Or *you*? I'll tell you. Out of workers. Out of people like me, that's how. Their life-blood. And you're grateful. For a few of her scrapings. Her eyes went to the clock: The kids'll be home any minute.

—Aren't you? Admit it. Grateful.

—With you out of work, I am.

31

His eyes blazed at her words.

—Off sick, then. I'm not saying it's your fault. She stepped down into the kitchen and put a kettle on. Humming. Picking out a plain sugar biscuit for herself.

—Get your son Edward out of school and we shouldn't need her dole, said her husband. Took out a diary from his pocket, and a yellow handkerchief. He wiped his head.

—Edward's not leaving school, cried Clara.

—You're a foolish, obstinate woman.

In his exasperation Peretz began to cough; hawking again and again into his handkerchief.

—What have I done to deserve it? he shook his head.

—Edward is staying on at school, Peretz.

—Oh, independent today, are you? One phone call. In how long, how many weeks? What do you think, your sister will let you move *in* with her?

He spat contemptuously.

—Look at yourself, Clara.

Half-unconsciously her eyes went to the mirror. Black eyes, still gentle, searched her own face.

—We've moved apart, she said: since Mother died. I know.

—Well, that's the understatement of the week.

—Yes, Clara swallowed: It wasn't obvious. In Brewer Street. How it was going to be. I remember Alex. Coming to the house then.

—Like a prince.

—Like you, said Clara quietly: Like you were, once.

3

—The Cloisters in Arles. Doorways, tympanums, mandala. A long walk between sea and salt for ten miles to *Les deux Saintes Maries*. And it's been very cold here, Tobias. Does that answer your question?
—Not in the least.

They were driving uphill away from the sea. Below them a single creek of blue could be glimpsed briefly between deep stones; then it vanished behind a windbreak of cypress trees. The air was bright, but the sun had a silvery pallor; the green of the winter leaves darkened in it. Between white slabs of stone, a few trees with bare branches, oaks mainly, had a glint of frost on them, and the occasional pile of brown leaves lay at their bole. Tobias looked unswervingly ahead. An aroma of lavender soap rose from him, as if he had just straightened up from a washbasin. His skin was so waxy smooth, it was impossible to imagine blue stubble pushing through it. And the thin triangle of his mouth, seen from the side, was set in a permanent cat's triangle of suppressed amusement. He had taken his hands out of his gloves, which lay folded tidily on the shelf in front of him, and his hands lay finger-tip to finger-tip in his lap. Mendez' sidelong glance met no response.
—Are you tired?
—I slept on the plane.

What was it he so resented? Mendez puzzled. What had he been dragged from? What would he rather have been doing?

—Have you brought your golf-clubs?

—No. I shan't be here more than a few days.

—Have I spoilt some arrangement, bringing you here this weekend?

—If I'd had an urgent appointment I should have told you. I hate putting things off.

—So. What are you brooding over? My state of mind?

—No. Since that's perfectly obvious, said Tobias: The château is now complete, isn't it? You haven't brought yourself to move in.

—How do you know the château is ready? It's very cold, said Mendez: especially on the stairs. All those stone flags.

—But you *have* paid the builders. And the architect.

—A few extra radiators, muttered Mendez pettishly: Tonight we are going to have dinner with a man who plays the flute beautifully. I wonder. You don't play anything, do you? Can you read the bass line on a piano?

—I doubt it.

—Try.

—And we visit the winter palace tomorrow?

Mendez thought; he has his finger on something. But he's likely to be wrong, whatever it is. Because he always reads his own soul into me. His own neat white soul. Oblong. For a moment Mendez speculated angrily on the debilitations of prudence. How well it worked for you, until the world went mad; how all the machinery of it foundered then, how easily all the ordinary detergents failed. All the dignity of prudent men depended on the sanity of the world around them. Fear? It was for burghers everywhere. They played safe to the end, bartering for their furniture first, and afterwards their lives. Hadn't he seen that? While others fought. His brothers. In silver birch-woods, killed in the first spring rain.

—I'll be delighted to show you my new home tomorrow,

Tobias, he said: Meanwhile aren't you pleased? To find me hobnobbing with my neighbours?

Mendez was dressed in a three-quarter-length fur overcoat, and a fur hat which covered his enormous head.

—You look very well, I admit, said Tobias abruptly.

—Yes? Let me tell you how I met this M. Benoit. It was on the quay at La Ciotat. First he was explaining to me about the true *Bouillabaisse*. Conger-eels, sea-perch, red mullet and hog-fish. (Those last evidently essential.) *Cigales de mer*, crab, lobster, crayfish —

—Alex, for pity's sake.

—Sweet peppers, shallots, fennel, bay leaves. And oil. The good rich oil of Provence. Magnificent, Tobias. Then, of course, after we had eaten, we played a Bach Chaconne.

—Of course. And did the other clients throw you francs?

—No, we were up in his flat by that time. M Benoit owns the restaurant. Naturally he prefers to live away from the coast.

Mendez turned the car abruptly into a smaller road, and smiled at his friend as he hunched deep into the tub seat, refusing to make his long legs more comfortable.

—You will like his village. It is very traditional. And the house looks like a run-down farmhouse. Last week, Mendez continued: I met a juggler. From Turkey. He had come south to Marseilles through Germany.

—I suppose he *juggled* beautifully?

—I think he may have been out of practice, said Mendez gravely: In Germany he had been working in a sausage factory for some time. In Turkey he had a wife and children; and he sent them money every week until last spring when one day he discovered they were dead.

—All of them?

—Perhaps he exaggerated a little.

—And what language did he use? To tell you all this.

—Now *that*, Tobias, not the juggling, was the true point of our relationship. He spoke only Turkish, as it happened. Perhaps you remember that on my way out of Odessa once I spent a short time in Istanbul.

—I don't remember. So. You speak Turkish.

—Just enough to understand his problem. You know the whores of Marseilles? said Mendez: Extraordinary. On the quayside of *le vieux port*, have you ever seen them? He wanted a black one. With long legs and the most brazen tits. Imagine. How could he approach them or bargain with them?

—Are you saying you negotiated a price? For him?

—Perhaps it is my métier? Anyway, I found it quite enjoyable.

—How completely disgusting, said Tobias, after a pause.

They drove a little way in silence. The sun was dropping. Long tree shadows made it difficult to avoid the stones in the road.

—Are you really such a prig? Mendez asked at last.

—I suppose you could hardly contain yourself from leaping after him? I think you should alert the police if you are going to take risks of that kind.

—What is such a risk? I understand, said Mendez. A little contempt came into his own voice: Tobias, you are a hypochondriac. About violence. Because you've never had the smell of it in your nose. When my father was sixty he could still look after himself. And *le vieux port*, in any case, is hardly dockside Marseilles.

—Your father, said Tobias: was probably worth about five roubles not five million. I am absolutely serious, Alex. You could be kidnapped, held to ransom. Don't laugh. There was a case only last week.

—A boy of eighteen, wasn't it?

—You aren't proof against sub-machine guns? Are you? Or is *that* a trick your father taught you in the villages of Byelorussie?

—No. That is a knack, said Mendez quietly : you could certainly say they did not have in the villages. On the other hand, with sub-machine guns, you know, Tobias, it is possible to remove anyone from anywhere.

—True, said Tobias.

—Now M. Benoit's house lies a little beyond here. Will you look out for a lane of cypress trees? The fields flatten first, I remember. Please don't sulk.

—Banal. Squalid, muttered Tobias : How can you behave with so little dignity?

—I like to. Sometimes. All right, I confess, said Mendez : of course I knew you'd hate that story. And that's why I told it. You shouldn't be so squeamish.

—Thank you, said Tobias : And this Benoit, what's he? For my education.

—I promise you'll like him, said Mendez : honestly, I'm sure of it. He is your true Provençal *bourgeois*. Everything in order; church on Sunday; careful and decent to the bone; without the least self-indulgence. Except perhaps in food. And. In any event.

—And?

—The questions that bother me won't worry you.

—Oh I see, said Tobias, the Occupation, you mean? Well, it would be very rude to go on about that.

—Very rude, agreed Mendez : Most uncivil.

—Don't you think? asked Tobias, staring.

They came out of the last wintry sunshine into an interior rich as a dark fruit; red tiles under foot; and a long oak table set with brightly coloured china. M. Benoit was a slight, neat man with a moustache and stooped

37

shoulders. As he led them in he said : I have no more a
wife. But a very good cook.

Tobias took in the order of the room with pleasure and
approval.

—You see, there is more to France than apéritifs and
tobacco-dens, said M. Benoit, with satisfaction.

From the trestle table rose the sweet tang of black
olives and fresh seed bread. On a wooden board were
three kinds of pâté; to one of which Benoit directed their
attention with a query in his voice : It is made from the
little bird. Thrushes, he said : Perhaps you don't like
that? Here it is traditional.

He said the last word as if it could be used to explain
a good deal. As they sat down about the table, a young,
plump, rather pert, young girl brought in one or two side
dishes. To judge from her flounce, and the way her eyes
sized up the guests she was not Benoit's mistress. Still,
Benoit's eyes watched her moodily as she left the room.

—I hope you like pheasant? I have a little land round
here. Good for olives, maybe, but not wine. You can
feel as much in your fingers. But for pheasants, he
laughed : You know I wish all tourists who come to
France knew our countryside. Our country people are
the only beautiful ones. If I had a son, I would give him
a farm, and I would have everything to make me happy.
My own few hectares, he said, go back two centuries.
Round here we have *honnêtes gens*, you know. We like
discipline, work and order.

The willing girl returned, with a dish of steaming birds,
their flesh dark, the sauce a deep red.

—Superb, said Mendez, with one eye on the girl's own
plumpness.

She flushed, but lifted her chin and returned his gaze
with a certain boldness.

—Magnificent, said Tobias.

38

Benoit poured wine for them proudly. He was pleased with his guests. Flattered by their presence.

—And M. Mendez, you see, he said. Where does he choose to come? To the *campagne*, naturally. He understands where the health of Europe is.

—I always considered him more a man of the cities, said Tobias mischievously.

—Of course, we are all men of the cities, what else can we be? I also have to spend weeks in Marseilles. But when it comes to choosing a home. Where else can you still find authority and hierarchy, and the basis of good life?

—I told you, said Mendez: that you would find yourself in good company, Tobias.

—But I'm not sure what I think, said Tobias: About Alex' choice of environment.

M. Benoit raised his eyebrows.

—For him, I mean, said Tobias: It seems to me quite possibly disabling. To try and change his natural relationship with—

—Power?

—Truly speaking, the whole geography of his success.

Mendez said, a little grimly: I trust *you* to keep me in touch.

—Then *you* must read my reports, said Tobias quickly.

M. Benoit, who had not followed the last exchange, nevertheless detected the note of it. And as the girl returned, carrying crystallized chestnuts, he watched their faces anxiously.

—Round here everything must be very much as it always was, Tobias remarked.

—Yes. For one thing, even now they don't like the English, Mendez teased him.

M. Benoit frowned at that.

—You remember Mers-el-Kebir? The British killed many hundreds of French sailors. Early in the war.

Because they don't trust. And some people like to remember these black pages. Not me, he said reproachfully: all my family round here always believe in a happy Europe.

—Always? asked Mendez, with a certain irony.

—All my life. I am not ashamed. There are other points of view; but, for me, the test was always God's will.

—*That's* always seemed to me the most difficult thing to sort out, said Mendez.

—Ah, perhaps. In some areas. But under *La Gueuse*, the old republic, *that* was a scandal, you know. There was absolutely *no* teaching of the Church in schools. It was forbidden. And after Pétain, only then, we had spiritual values; the family; fecundity. He put a stop to moral decadence. Of course, when they begin to send good French workmen to their German factories who can support such a government? But we try not to think of such times.

—Some people, I suppose, might have objected a little before? asked Alex gently.

—I don't think so. Those first laws were against foreigners. Only. Not racist laws, as I see you think. No. I think we even consulted the Vatican. But, of course, when the Germans came in 1942 it was quite a different matter.

But as he took a piece of bread, which he clearly had no intention of eating, both Alex and Tobias observed that his hand was shaking, and that he did not carry the bread to his lips. Tobias turned the direction of the conversation quickly: The woman who owned Alex' château during the war. She would be part of a great family from round here, I suppose?

At once M. Benoit's blue eyes lost their cloud and his mouth thinned with precision: Not at all. A family of small town lawyers from the west. *Métèques*, certainly.

—In England they told me she was some kind of Resistance heroine.

—*Métèques?* asked Mendez, frowning.

—Is a word of Maurras. I am not a poet, you know, perhaps it is an ugly word. It means half-breeding, yes.

For the first time he looked rather narrowly at his new friends : Yes, it is an ugly word. Well, I help many, many of them. And war veterans, you know, were all exempt from any restraints. I mean.

There was an uncomfortable pause.

—I think, said Tobias : I should like to hear the music I have been promised. I see you have a fine harpsichord, M. Benoit.

—It has a lovely tone, M. Benoit agreed. But without animation. None of them moved from the table. M. Benoit still seemed rather disturbed.

—You know, he said : perhaps the lady hid a few refugees who were waiting for visas and boats. I only saw her go by from time to time. She walked very proudly, and she was a stranger, as I say. Also, I am sorry to say it, but she slept with many many people. Many kinds, you know. I was sorry she should be shot, but she was not so young. And to my view at least, not exactly a Jeanne d'Arc.

—That's fascinating, said Tobias : And now.

—Your flute, said Mendez.

The man rose with an abrupt motion, and wiped his lips with a red linen cloth.

—Yes, yes, he agreed : there are too many ghosts. Let them go.

As Benoit began to assemble his flute, and Mendez flicked through a book of Telemann sonatas, Tobias glanced idly at the local Provençal paper. The front page headlined the story of a mysterious burglar-blonde who was apparently defeating the Marseilles police by refusing to give her name. Under French law a person without a name, the journal explained with evident

41

enjoyment, cannot be made to stand trial or be sentenced. On the other hand, as a method of defence Tobias saw it had its drawbacks. The police did appear able to hold you in custody for some time. It seems she was alleged to have broken into a private house near Aix.

Tobias looked at the photograph. It was taken in an unprepossessing attitude, with both arms folded under breasts that were barely visible. The blondeness of the hair would certainly have to be taken on trust, since there was no lustre in the photograph. She was wearing dark glasses; and her face had that dumb expressionless look produced by a cheap flash in a station kiosk. There was, however, something familiar about it. The mouth; a certain relationship of bones in the cheeks, a certain flare in the nostrils.

Tobias felt the beginning of excitement. He turned back, to read the paragraphs he had skipped. The girl was aged about thirty, with a slight accent, but the police were not certain whether she was really a foreigner, or only affecting to be so. They were investigating if she was British. A police inspector was on record as saying she *looked* English.

Tobias looked back again at the expressionless picture; and was not sure. Could this really be the face in the broken silver frame he had seen on Oliver Walsh's floor? It seemed unlikely.

The two instruments, flute and recorder, had begun to weave a pattern of such delicious jarring notes about his senses, that together with the good red wine, he felt a little light-headed. He turned, nevertheless, to the back page of the paper for further information.

A man was said to have been with her when she was arrested. He had escaped through a window of the house. Naturally the police had checked her fingerprints and other personal details without turning up any criminal record.

Without really thinking about it, Tobias slid a cigarette from Mendez' packet and lit it.

—Tobias, called Mendez : you promised us a bass line.

—I'm sorry.

—Put out your cigarette, come on. What are you reading?

Tobias brought the newspaper over to the two men : I'm fascinated by your legal system, he said neutrally, holding out the photograph towards them.

—*Blonde Inconnue*, M. Benoit read aloud.

Mendez looked at it longer : They aren't going to get much response if they go around printing photographs like that. She could be anyone in Europe. In dark glasses. And her hair drawn back. They must be stupid. Or corrupt. Actually, she reminds me of a singer I listened to on the pavements of Aix about a month ago.

Ah, said Tobias, relieved : how interesting. She reminded *me* of Walsh's sister. You know, the bloke whose mother owned your château.

—Let me look, said M. Benoit. He wrinkled his glasses up his nose, and peered down the thicker part of the lens. His face was unreadable.

—Well?

—It could be anybody, I should agree.

—I suppose so.

—So come on, said Mendez : Look. Your part is very simple. Six or seven notes. A child of seven could do it.

—Yes. All the same, said Tobias quietly : I think I shall pay a visit to Aix police station. Tomorrow afternoon. Just a professional curiosity, of course.

4

Down Charlotte Street the pavement was covered with
greenish sludge, with pieces of blue tissue and straw
from fruit shops lying in it. Passing the open stalls,
Lalka caught the smell of mushrooms, oil-heating and
unseasonable flowers. She placed her small feet delicately.
She was humming. What a febrile thing, I am, she
thought. Up and down. This morning playing the piano.
Deliberately choosing a piece Alex loved. Playing on
and on until the pain of it smarted in her eyes, and
the salt in her throat made it hard to swallow. And then.
Crying, almost with pleasure, she had taken up a piece
of Chopin and begun again. Her fingers remembering,
flying. In sudden joy. And when she finished, flushed,
there was Alex' mocking voice in her head : You see?
You're better off without me. Aren't you? We never
really liked the same things.

Well, she *would* surprise him, that was something, she
thought. Surprised at the intensity of that desire. How
she had wondered once. *What* could do it? She had
wracked her brains thinking. Lovers? He'd expected
them. Not bothering? He could accommodate that. And
then suddenly, to be given an opportunity. On a plate.
As if it were some kind of gift from God. Yes, she could
hardly wait to give him the news, now she had decided,
because she knew, he would never understand. She still
trembled herself at the thought of it. To go off. Just like
that. Almost in disguise. Well. Travelling *poor*, as Katie

put it. It was that phrase had decided her. She could never have gone back. Not there, not to Krakow, never, not like a rich American tourist to gawk about the floodlit Rynek. How could she walk between the lovely old houses where all her mother's friends had lived; Halina and Tadeuz, Jerzy, the Bobrowskis; she had heard their names through her childhood like a *kaddish*. And she knew the town itself was untouched, not like Warsaw; even the buildings of Kasimiersh. But the old stalls, and the Jews with their tooled leather shops, and brass wear, and small bargains – everyone came across Krakow to Kasimiersh for bargains – all the stall were gone. The bustle, and the smells, and the seeds of sunflowers spilt in the streets. Yes everything had been tidied away, all that. She knew. And the borders. She was still a little afraid of borders. Couldn't she still smell the hay-cart she had hidden in crossing south all those years ago? How could people fly in, rich now, as if nothing had happened?

But to go back second-class rail; to stay in some poet's flat out of town; in a block of cheap new flats that hadn't even existed before; that was all right. That was something else. When Mendez phoned she would say: By the way, I'm off in the middle of January.

And then for a moment she experienced a treacherous and irrelevant hope. Perhaps he would be afraid for her? What would I do, she wondered, if he said, Lalka, please don't go. It's dangerous. Come back to me instead?

At once she dismissed the fantasy. Daydreams. How hard they were to fight off these days. She had walked out of the house into the cold to escape the trance of one; and even now with white rain blowing flat into her face she had nearly fallen back into another.

And she was early for Katie. Early altogether. The small room, usually packed with noisy people, looked

45

oddly desolate. She wondered, with a little resentment, how late Katie would be. Wasn't she always late? It didn't matter. Except that it left time. For tricks of memory. Flick Flick.

—A glass of burgundy.

Flick. She had read about the patients with sleeping sickness woken with L-Dopa. All their life has run by, and then flick, flick, they were awake. But possessed with terrible images. She thought: I have been sleep-walking all my life; and now here they come, the terrible images, the discontinuous film-strip; the dream of hope; the sudden violence.

Once Alex had affectionately put his hand to her throat as they slept, and she had screamed: Don't!

And he woke up very offended: What's the matter? You can't think I wanted to strangle you?

—Of course not, she said, too quickly. Drawing her shoulders in, protectively. Turning away. Of course, but what then? Why had she felt so exposed, so helpless? The veins in her neck seemed to throb with the memory of violence. Even the nerves at the back of her ears.

And he shook her shoulder angrily: You should see a doctor.

—All right.

And then he lay on his back and looked up at the ceiling: Mind you, I'm not sure you can be *helped* if you refuse to remember anything.

She was still defensive: It's all bunk. Anyway. Everyone forgets those first years.

—No. I can remember a lot.

—Before you were six?

The birds were singing. The green tree-light came into

the slope of his room, and lit their ceiling with circles of watery shadows. She turned back towards him.

—I'll have another glass of wine.

Blast. Where was Katie. The waiting was unspeakable. How could she stay in the present? She was lost. Straw between bare feet, relaxing. Stepping on sharp pebbles, on some bleak northern beach; happily in love with a cousin who taught her to harden the soles of her feet by walking on pebbles. Lalka wondered what had happened to him.

And shook her head. Would it be like this to be a widow? Better or worse? People would be more embarrassed by her, of course. You would frighten them. And you were just as alone. With the same voices banging inside your head. Only pride was salved. But what mercy was that? For the first time she asked herself the question. How would she feel if Mendez was dead? And for a moment, a vicious pleasure suffused and horrified her. She couldn't believe it. Really? Did she feel *so* humiliated?

But then the thought of his body being hurt in any way entered her imagination. She couldn't bear it. He staggered about ill in her mind until she almost had to cover her eyes against the vividness of the fear. That even a momentary ill-wishing could harm him. Silently, at her table, she called back her thought. She blessed him, hysterically. Was she going mad?

Meanwhile, the voice of memory continued.

—You say I destroy *you*, I deny *your* internal life. How? Alex, only tell me *how*? God knows you eat away at mine.

—But what *is* that? How can I know? You keep it so hidden. I want to live with someone who's part of the outside world. I can't live in one room cells. We have set up one-room cells all over the world.

Then she had beaten at him with her nails, and he had not understood why. It was truly as if she didn't exist for him. He never even knew when he hurt her most.

Once. Yes. She had been so miserable she had rung him at work. Knowing she would only get through to a cool female voice saying: Is that his wife?

And always Lalka hated to admit it.

—Shall I connect you? They're all at a meeting, you know.

What desperation made her agree that time? He had sounded so bewildered: What? Is anything wrong?

—I just. Wanted to apologize. For the way.

—But didn't they tell you I'm in conference?

—Yes. I just was so unhappy about. This morning.

And he'd forgotten the whole thing. All their quarrel. Now it was only ringing up was the offence. That became the embarrassment. How remote he was from her in his male world and yet, wasn't it *he* who said: Lalka, you are so hidden. So hidden.

Well, now at last that was true. She *was* hidden. She had put away everything she felt. Put it away. Never would she speak about her pain to anyone. Least of all Katie. Never. It was all locked up tight and sometimes she even forgot about it herself. Didn't she?

—Lalka! I'm so sorry. Am I awfully late? Will you forgive me? I've had the most *horrible* morning.

There she was. Katie. Under her huge velvet hat, with its floppy brim, her dark face looking like a parody of Bloomsbury. She had to keep the hat on with one hand and peer a little from underneath. Still, it suited her.

And she hadn't spoken loudly, but a few people sitting down turned round to watch her arrival speculatively.

Lalka herself felt the change in the room's vitality as if she had been miraculously restored to her own flesh. She had been sitting limply, and now her muscles regained their tone; the spirit returned to her face. She felt herself physically becoming the Lalka Katie knew; a different self from the slack mind-wandering person she was alone. Both women laughed.

—What are you drinking? asked Katie: No. I need something stronger.

—As bad as that? Lalka's voice lifted into teasing.

—It's such a ridiculous story. What shall we have? This place is Greek isn't it? Have you ordered? Let's have houmous and one of those vineleaf rolls, and what are they called? Those slabs of bread.

—Why are you so agitated?

—Well, it's partly running around arranging visas. Katie's face shone when she laughed: No, it's awful. I don't think I can tell *anyone* the truth any more. Lalka, would you say I was furtive?

Lalka eyed her sceptically: Not in any usual sense.

—Exactly. Now I spent yesterday afternoon propping up Johnnie. Remember him? He's supposed to be a composer? He's got this job at a posh school. Christ knows how. Anyway. You won't believe this, but somehow the whole term no one discovered he couldn't play the piano. But yesterday someone presented the school with a marvellous Steinway. Oh God. What an optimist. You know what he did? He suddenly seized up with cramp in his right hand! I mean it. There's the whole bloody school sitting out front waiting to hear his piece and he's staggering about with a crooked wrist like something out of a horror movie. Saying: It's come on me. The pain. I can't do it. I can't do it!

49

Katie mimed.

—And could he?

—Absolutely he *couldn't*. Everyone more or less died with embarrassment. And, of course, he was fired, on the spot. So I gave him some money. Not much. But that's not the point. That isn't the end of the story. Tell me, do you think I ought to have mentioned it? I mean to —

—Your husband? Don't go on. It might have been wiser. Oh, Katie.

—Yes. I can see that now. But I can't seem to explain. To anyone. How I've been conditioned *not* to. I mean, remember all that fuss about taxis we had? Last month. Think of that.

—Yes, but don't you remember? It was the same thing. It was because you didn't *ask*.

—Well, fuck it. He looks like a benevolent uncle too, doesn't he? Why should I always *ask* everything? I'm not used to it. Anyway if that was dishonest, I'm dishonest. I can't help it.

—I don't blame him looking out for it.

—Listen, you're wrong. Do you know I've been totally faithful? Every so often I thought, you know, this one. Maybe it'll really work? And today he says I'm the shiftiest, most evasive bitch he's ever known. Take that in.

—Come on, you're exaggerating.

—No. That's why I'm late. I mean, I had to reply, didn't I?

—Katie, why don't you just *tell* him whatever it is?

—Well, I *do* if he asks. Only how can I *think* of everything he's going to find a sign of unspeakable treachery?

—I meant. Just tell the truth.

—Oh, it's so easy for you. Where is this food, I'm ravenous. I don't know how you do it. Christ, I envy you, Lalka. The way you sit, the way you cross your legs. You're so bloody quiet. And tough. Everyone thinks *I'm* tough because I keep making a noise; but it's just because I'm so miserable I could weep.

Irritably Katie put out half a cigarette. Caught the expression on Lalka's face, and began to laugh.

—What do you do all day, Lalka? Aren't you bored?

—Sometimes. Aren't you?

—Of course so am I. Bored I mean. But I can't understand why you aren't desperate all the time. The same way.

—To *achieve* something, you mean? Well, I don't know what it would *be*, I suppose.

—You haven't any kids.

—No.

—Do you mind? Oh, don't answer that. It's not the point; I've got three; all different, lovely things; and I *still* go on getting things off. Getting things *done*. It's almost degrading.

Lalka turned down her mouth and shrugged: I suppose I haven't your energy. Or talent.

—But I'm exhausted. I have to sleep nine hours a night or I'm collapsing. And as for talent.

—Yes?

—Well, I haven't *done* anything yet, whatever it is. And I'm not likely to now. Look, I'm a journalist. I do features. So the fuck what?

Lalka shook her head. None of it had any meaning for her. It was nothing she'd ever wanted. The by-lines, the public name. They began eating.

—Do you know the worst thing I ever did? said Katie through a mouthful of finely shredded cabbage: Now listen to this, and you'll see how far out these bastards are. The very worst thing? Lalka said: Why tell me?

—Guilt, darling, guilt. Listen. And, Christ, look out for those pickled chilis. They're vicious.

—I like them.

—Listen. I stole a man's life. Once. He just trusted me, and I did that to him. He met me in a bar and chatted me up and I listened like I was a pretty little hen-brain and then I wrote it all up. Everyone said I was a lucky girl. *Lucky.* I mean, imagine. I just work my ass off all my life trying to get one foot in the door, and then I do something really shitty like that and they say *lucky girl.*
—He must have been pretty famous.
—Yes. Well. I guess you never read my paper or you'd know about it. Anyway. That's the worst thing I ever did.
—It doesn't sound so bad, laughed Lalka.
—It was bad. Let's have another bottle.

But Lalka was staring down at her left hand. Her face changed, white, damp with horror.
—What's the matter?

On the third finger of Lalka's left hand, above the platignum circlet that would not come off, four claw feet bent over an oblong space.
—Look. She held out her hand.

Katie too stared at the huge oblong space : What a size. What was it?
—A sapphire.
—Well, I guess it might have been a diamond. Was it insured?
—I suppose so. Oh, that's not the point. Lalka was so miserable she could hardly keep back the tears. The sudden loss was like a comment on the whole false camaraderie, the bogus self she had been sustaining in Katie's presence. Because the sapphire was her engagement ring. And to have lost it was suddenly unbearable.
—One of the claws is defective, said Katie.
—Yes. Yes. I see that now.

The ring bought in Brighton twenty years ago, with Alex holding Clara on one arm, and Lalka on the other.

Like a huge big brother. Handsome. Just back from the desert. After the war, of course, it was after the war, but the beaches were still wired weren't they? All she could remember was how the three of them had staggered along the front, drunk with beer and youth, and smelled seaspray and seaweed. And laughed. How old was Clara? Not more than fifteen. And when Alex had seen the second-hand jewelry shop, all three had gone quiet, and looked. What an absurd purchase. Then. He had spent every pound in his wallet and afterwards had to hitch back to his unit.

—Look at the glow in it, Clara had said.

—You don't think it's vulgar? It's so big.

Certainly it was bigger than any ring anyone else ever had in Brewer Street. Usually they went in for little chips of diamond.

—How can a jewel like that be vulgar?

Clara so young then and without envy. Lalka remembered how she'd kissed them both.

—Be happy now, she warned them: But you must be. You're both so beautiful.

—You weren't listening, accused Katie.

5

—I hope you don't expect me to be grateful. I was quite enjoying it. In gaol.

In spite of fatigue, and faint blue shadows under her eyes, the girl's features retained their high-boned beauty. Her lips were white, her hair the colour of pale string. She looked round the long room, with its long windows, velvet curtains, restored stucco, and comfortable couches and said pertly: You've certainly tarted this place up, haven't you?

—I'm sorry if the changes upset you, said Mendez formally.

—Why? Because of my mother you mean? She laughed: That bitch. I wonder what became of her bedroom furniture?

—Oh, said Mendez awkwardly: I think it's still here somewhere. If you would like to have it.

—God, no. I just wondered if you'd succumbed to all the frills and twirls. Have you re-built the kitchen?

—I'll show you, if you like. It's not so changed.

—The sounds are different in this room, she muttered: Less *hollow* somehow. Oh, now I see. You've lowered the ceiling, haven't you? She looked round: Where does the heat come from?

—Under the floor.

—Does this room still lead to the terrace? Can I look?

Without waiting for permission, she drew the heavy curtain. Outside it was cloudy and dark; the glass became

54

a black mirror as she stared out. Shrugged. Moved away. And let the room replace her image, so that the paintings and china seemed to hang outside warmly and richly in the dark, in the trees.

—Home, she said with disgust: Why do rich people always want to make homes for themselves? Families are so disgusting. They pull one another to pieces.

—As it happens, I live alone.

—But you can't help making it comfortable, can you? She laughed. It was an inconsequent, prolonged giggle, without apparent relevance.

—Do you like the fireplace at least? asked Mendez. He was a little proud of it, having found it in a run-down farmhouse just west of Vauvenargues.

—It's all right.

—Too fancy?

—No. I said. It's all right. I just don't get very excited by objects.

—Except to steal them? inquired Tobias.

He had been sitting, a silent presence, throughout the conversation. She swung upon him with immediate hostility, and then dropped her eyes under his cool stare.

—I want a bath, she said: Have you got my bag? Or is it in the car?

—It's been put upstairs for you.

She pointed over the fireplace.

—You've brought back the Fragonard.

—Your brother sold it, said Tobias.

—I bet he cheated you then, she said.

Tobias smiled: I let him think so.

—Isn't he a shit? she asked conversationally: Just like my father. I suppose you can understand my mother not caring what happened to her can't you?

—I understand she took a lot of risks for other people, said Mendez.

55

—Oh, the war was a godsend for her. She always liked taking risks. Whatever else, she wasn't cosy.

—Cosiness can be very alarming, agreed Mendez.

She looked at him, surprised.

—Small homes, small rooms. Small-scale pleasures. Like love. Happiness. They're particularly vulnerable. But you're young to write them off.

—I like to have everything I need in a bag I can carry, she said : That's the only real way to be safe.

—Sometimes even a bundle is too much. Even your clothes or your body, said Mendez.

She bit her lip. For a moment the lines from her nose to mouth were visible.

—Yes. I suppose so. Whyever did you buy this fortress then ? If you know all that.

Mendez rang a bell on a long velvet cord : That's my business.

—You've made it work ! She clapped her hands : It never used to.

—Go upstairs, said Mendez : Your jeans are torn, and your feet are dirty. Change. Then we'll have dinner. Do you like quails ?

She hesitated : You don't object to having a burglar in your house ?

—Unlike my friends, said Mendez : whose Moustier china you broke on your way down the rope ladder, what I most value is *not* portable.

The girl left and Tobias rose and began to pace up and down the room.

—What do your think ? asked Alex.

—Of your *home* ? Tobias inflected the word maliciously. Not much. Might be anywhere. St John's Wood, say.

---Really ? But I meant the girl. Why did you bring her

here? asked Mendez: To unsettle me? What? Sentiment? Spite? Or could it be, he suggested mildly: the Ansel loins have been touched with just the faintest tinge of ordinary human lust?

—It was pure curiosity.

—Pure?

—It's such a desolate time of year, said Tobias restlessly: I can't imagine why anyone would come and live here in the winter. For choice.

—Well, at least there's no rain. And no fog, said Mendez cheerfully: It's healthy.

—Just blank dry darkness, Tobias said moodily: with trees, like bones trailing hair. Everyone to their taste, I suppose.

Lee came down in white muslin, caught on a ribbon under her almost invisible breasts. Her hair hung forward, and the slight puffiness had gone from her eyelids. She still wore no make-up – perhaps she had none with her – and the only colour in her face shone from her eyes, in which the blue seemed to have darkened.

—Transfigured, she said. Turning for them: But it's too early for dinner. What shall we do?

—I could show you round, said Mendez, diffidently: if that wouldn't bore you. The building isn't finished, of course.

—Can we go up the tower?

—Yes. Right to the top if you like.

Her eyes lit with malice: And you aren't afraid of dragons and flying serpents?

—None of the workmen observed any. But you aren't wearing shoes.

—I'll put some on. I've some plimsolls. Wait.

The stone flags of the stairs were untouched, and Mendez was right; the heating did not quite cope with the upward spiral of cold air. She shivered a little. Mendez took off his jacket.

—Here.

As they mounted, Mendez' own shoes clopped on the stone like a horse, and the girl's were silent. It was an odd sensation, as if he were climbing beside a ghost.

—Are you puffed? he asked, to break the silence.

—No. I could run up if I wanted.

—And the height doesn't make you nervous?

They came out on to a square turret, where the squares of a fortified parapet had been restored with new stone. Even in the dark it was possible to see an immense distance. The hillside, cut sharp against the sky, and, below, the shapes of half-seen trees, and fallen stones; even the lost village. Beyond that, a river flattened out towards the horizon.

—You're quite safe, said Alex.

—As a child, she said crisply : I climbed across from those tiles right over the old ballroom. Are you going to restore that?

—You can see in a few minutes.

—Look at those old houses. Did you know the people over there live on beans? And lentils?

—No one lives there now.

She fell silent : The *santons*? Do you like them?

—They're still there. Yes. But they remind me of Poland. Except in Poland, Mendez corrected : there are more martyrdoms and crucifixions than Christmas cribs. You're shivering. Shall we go in?

—Wait a moment more. I see you've had people at work in the gardens. How hopeless !

—They are planting black cherries, said Mendez.

—They won't prosper. Nothing grows on this hillside.
She laughed.
—And you've put in a Roman fountain. Poor Mendez.
A fountain!
—That will work. Don't worry, said Mendez: the water
will run from the mains. Tell me. We have met before,
haven't we? In Aix? You begged a light from me.
—Really. I can't remember.

On the way down the stairs she paused.
—This room. It was my mother's. Did you know? Is
that why you haven't opened it?
—No. There are many rooms unopened. If you like, you
may have one.
—This one?
Mendez turned her towards him quietly in the soft
light. He lifted her chin and looked into her eyes. Then
he put one hand on her miniscule breast. His own breath
came a little more quickly. She did not move.
—Any you like, he said.
She turned, and they went on walking downwards.
—Very well. You must let me take you round the garden.
—But it's dark. No moon. And cold. Later on, said
Mendez, a little crossly: I shall have some floodlights
put in.
—But it's not raining, she said. For a moment her voice
sounded almost gay: We'll both put coats on.
—All right.
At the next turn of the stairs he said: This leads to the
library. If you're interested.
She hesitated, and he opened the door. In a kind of daze,
her eyes went round the tiers of books in their lines
against the walls.
—My God. So this is what you've done with the ball-

room. Have you read all these? Or do you just collect them?

—I trail them through my mind, he said.

—I'm sorry. She flushed : That was rude.

—Why? You know who I am, said Mendez quietly : You recognized me in Aix. Didn't you? I'm an old dealer in diamonds. Fit to rob. Or. What else should you expect?

—My mother had all her parties here, the girl's voice rose joyfully : For everyone. Yes, even the Gestapo, though they didn't mention that when they gave us the medal. Here she sailed. In her old silks and wigs. And everyone caught at her skirts for a look or a touch.

—You can't have been more than three. What can you know?

—I can still smell her clothes. Well, and I remember her babble. Now there are books. All these books. What are they? Let me see?

—I'll put on more light, he said.

She gasped, as he pressed the switch. Looking upward.

—The glass. Now that she would have loved. Where did you find them?

—They are Austrian crystal. Do you like them?

—How old are they? Never mind. She brushed the pleasure aside : Let me see the books. It's like a university. Do these ladders slide along?

—If you like. I suppose you went to college, Lee?

—Yes, but they threw me out. It was very boring.

With one switch he illuminated the sections closest to them. She walked along them curiously.

—Maimonides. Mendelssohn. She touched the heavy leather books with their big square letters.

—And these are Hebrew. It means something to you, then, being a Jew?

—I don't know what it means. Something. Yes. But I expect that would be very boring, he said ironically.

—You mean all the camps and tortures? The six million dead? Yes, I can't help that. It's like the trenches. In the first war. I know with my head, but it doesn't affect me. I've heard it too often to feel it.

—Not real pain, you mean, like Vietnam, Biafra, Bangladesh?

—Well, they're *now*, aren't they? That's different.

—It all has to be news, he said, for your generation.

—Well, but to you it's *still* news. That's all the difference. Are you a Zionist?

—I'm a European, he said heavily.

—So am I, she said vigorously: I love Europe. I've lived in Berlin, Paris, Rome, everywhere. I hardly ever go back to England.

—But you're only skating, he shook his head: over the top soil.

—Well, I don't want to dig up the whole bloody graveyard, thank you. What about your friend Ansel?

—Oh, *he* is English to the marrow.

—But Jewish too?

—Why don't you ask him, people mean different things.

In the silent room, the quiet thud of a book being closed startled her. For a moment she looked afraid: Is there someone else here?

A familiar, pale-faced figure rose from behind the bookshelves to their right and announced gaily: I thought this might be a good moment to announce my presence. Always a problem, isn't it? Well, here I am. I must say it isn't my idea of a place for a good read, though, Alex. Don't you find it a trace oppressive?

—I hope you found what you were looking for nevertheless, said Mendez.

—Of course. Don't worry, I located your index system.

Very methodical, said Tobias : Who designed it for you?

—Show me your book, said Alex good-naturedly.

—Never mind about that. It will serve until dinner, and that's all it's good for. Are you staying on? Tobias asked Lee politely : You could continue your studies.

—I've no idea what I'm doing.

—No plans?

She flushed : None. Whatsoever.

—Well, except, said Alex gently : a turn in the garden. Lee turned to him gratefully : Of course. I'd forgotten.

There were no stars. The land dipped downward towards a grove of gnarled cypress trees. They stumbled on the scattered stones, Mendez at first supported her, but soon began to follow her lead; between the stones and the cut stumps. Under his feet the last year's leaves crunched. With frost. He shivered in the cold. They went between tangled twigs, under the flattened boughs of a cedar, deeper, the path sloping downwards, to a bridge. Over pebbles, though there was a trickle of invisible water. Overhead the evergreen foliage seemed poisonous. Dusty.

There was a sudden crack of guns. Then another. A few dogs began to bark.

—What's that? asked Mendez involuntarily.

—Poachers?

A scream of wild birds echoed from the south.

—Neighbours, I suppose, said Mendez uncertainly, knowing of none.

—Do you like the spirit of the forest you have bought?

—I am not afraid of spirits.

—Not even my poor mother's?

—People live as they must.

—Well, I *am* afraid of her.

—Then why have you come back here?

—I was *brought*, remember?

—Let me take your hand. That well-shaft is nearby. And the gate is rotten, the damned wood is going. Look. There.

—I think she wanted to be a saint, said Lee : Shall I tell you her story?

—If you know it. No one truly knows the story of their parents. And saying as much, Mendez tasted birchwoods in the rain, northern birch, silver.

—When I was young my father left ten children to bring me out of danger. Now they are dead. And I don't know *their* story, he murmured.

Perhaps she didn't hear. At any rate, she broke suddenly into wild, frenetic laughter.

—I think this bloody wood is toxic I must have it chopped down, muttered Mendez, his own flesh creeping : What's the matter with you?

Suddenly she seemed tired. She shivered : I've never known, really. Shall we go back to the house?

In the darkness the high towers looked taller than ever. A light left on in an upstairs room lit their path, and seemed to glower at them like an eye. Mendez found himself thinking they presented a perfect target for a gunman in just such a window, high up, as they traced their steps back along the ribbon of light.

Dinner was a meal morosely eaten, at least by Mendez and the girl, who seemed to have fallen into separate inturned pools of silence. Tobias, on the other hand, was unusually animated. Even in the yellow glow of the candlelight his eyes had an almost ferocious glitter. When Mendez refused potatoes he observed at once, sharply : I see. And which is it, Alex? Vanity or indigestion?

—Thank you, said Mendez. My belly is unchanged. In or out.

—Then you have some banal disease of the spirit, said Tobias : which is more disgusting.

As Mendez did not take him up, he continued : Poor Alex. Anyone who tries to avoid boredom with enough desperation always suffers from the same predictable diseases of repetition. This table, this excellent food, this superb wine. Notwithstanding.

—You seem to be enjoying them.

—Yes, but I come as a visitor. And tomorrow I shall be back to London very happily at work. Which you miss.

—What a rude man you are, said Lee, after a pause in which Mendez made no reply.

—You flatter him, said Alex : The truth is that this castle and probably you in it together alarm him, and he is looking for an excuse to leave.

Tobias raised his glass : Good.

He looked at Lee quizzically.

—I am sorry to have disappointed you, she said.

—Perhaps you could redeem yourself. I understand from the police you sing with great aplomb. You might do us an odd number. After the caramel.

—Should I? Would you like that? She asked Mendez.

—Tobias, said Alex : go to bed.

—Oh I intend to. Without coffee, if you'll excuse me. I've left you a report, by the way. On a table in your library. If I don't see you in the morning, Miss Walsh, would you like me to bear any message to your family?

—Tell them to rot, she said shortly.

—Without fail, he said courteously.

Lee moved her chair closer to Mendez.

—Why do you employ that vicious man?

Mendez looked up, for a moment puzzled: Does he worry you? He's always like that.

—And why are you so sad? she asked him: Do you miss your wife? I saw her in a magazine once. She is very lovely.

—Odd, I *was* thinking of her, he said, surprised: How strange of you to know. I should really write her a letter. Or phone.

—You are separated, aren't you?

—Yes, yes. But after all these years, he muttered.

—I understand. Lee put her hand on his neck, and left it there though he did not react or turn to her.

—I will come to your room tonight. Would you like that? she said quietly.

—Well, I'm not sure, said Mendez, apologetically. He did not mean to be ungracious; and she seemed not to be offended.

—Yes, she insisted: I want to come.

—Very flattering, said Mendez: but you might have done better with Ansel. He's younger, thinner in the hips, and with some peculiar interest in you. Which you may have missed.

—I know all about that.

—Another glass of wine? Mendez stalled moodily: It's early.

—Not now.

—So here you sleep. What a fantastic mirror, she said. Mendez too admired it, and intended some time to have a good local expert explain it to him. The three panels of glass were set in an unusual gilt frame in which half-clothed ladies, wild beasts and emblems unknown to him, were woven together in an arch of extraordinary grace. No doubt it was a copy of some more famous, possibly

Bacchic, orgy; but the effect was strangely innocent. The slender limbs of the ladies were not cast into lecherous attitudes, and the wild beasts were mostly drowsing or stretching peaceably.

—It came with the house, he said simply.

—No. I should have remembered it.

—Yes it was here, he said.

—The bed is new, anyway, she said mischievously : Four-poster. English. Like Henry VIII.

She undressed quietly, and threw her clothes over a chair. Then she approached like a thin wild animal and Mendez experienced a certain chill. She was not his physical type. He liked breasts, thighs, and a well-marked waist. To his surprise she knelt in front of him.

—What are you doing? Passive, and alarmed a little by the role, he let her take off his trousers without protest : Why are you pretending? You are doing this to arouse yourself, he muttered.

—So?

Against his will, her voice, and its hint of lascivious experience, had brought all his blood down to his bare, surprised penis. She held it gently between her hands as if blessing his body. Or bewitching it. Held it to her lips.

—What are you? he muttered. Harlot? Witch?

And pulled her upright.

—I'm too old to roll around on a stone floor.

—Are you?

But he seized her thin shoulders. She was not strong. Not difficult to carry.

—Pretend I'm a boy, a little boy, she whispered : Look. I'll lie flat on the bed, and you won't be able to tell the difference. I've no hips. Lie on me. *On* me.

Her long white back squirmed. Her eyes were shut. She moaned.

—Come on.

66

—For God's sake turn over, said Mendez.
She opened her eyes and raised her head: You insist on the missionary position? she mocked him.
—Not necessarily. But I do like to see who I'm fucking.
She laughed: That's rather sweet, you're rather sweet, she said.
He caressed her tentatively.
—No, don't bother with my tits. They aren't sensitive. They just aren't an erogenous zone as far as I'm concerned. Look.
    She led his hand down between her legs.
—That's where I like to be felt. Her voice dropped huskily: What do you like?
—You're so definite, said Mendez perplexed: I'm not sure you need me at all. You could just masturbate while I watched.
—Why? Don't you want to do it? She propped herself on one elbow: Don't worry, I won't be offended. I'll go back and sleep in the other room. If you don't want me.
—Shut up, he said: Just shut up. Can you?

Afterwards she lay smiling up at the ceiling as if she had accomplished something very important.

Mendez woke, wet and uncomfortable, less than an hour later, from a confused dream of hiding in a forest; of white rain; and the scuffle of men and voices. Warsaw had fallen. That much was clear. It was no longer a question of survival. The voices about him were unbroken, childish voices. He was with his brothers. Among the partisans. Unafraid. Blessed. Euphoric with the desire for resistance. Arguing only how to fight without weapons.

67

The light was still on as he woke out of the legend. And he had a sharp pain in his belly. He belched. Bloody Tobias. He rubbed his belly. Yes, he had indigestion. He would have to get up and find his tablets. Cautiously he disentangled his limbs from those of the girl on the bed, as he fumbled for his jacket and buttoned it dyspeptically.

The lines were gone from her face. Her lips, slightly parted, had the expression of someone also lost in dreaming. He would have liked to read her dream. Was that some triumph in her lips? Certainly she enjoyed sex; his mouth pursed in puzzled memory of that. But no sign remained of it in her sleeping face. Chaste and sleeping, she looked like an early Mary receiving the Annunciation with a breathless sense of miracle.

He scratched his head, looking down at her; almost tempted to wake her, with some blundering accusation. But supposing she held out her arms again? He got back between the sheets and firmly extinguished the light.

6

The winter morning lay blank on the mat. Nothing. Not so much as a bill. No letter from Mendez. Lalka thought, Of course. People he no longer sees just go right out to the edges of his thought and drop over. Into blackness. Haven't I seen that time and again? What a fool I was to forget. She shivered in the cold light that fell over her from the snow sky outside. Through the long windows she could see the canvas hood of a sports car glittering white with frost. And every cell in her blood clamoured: stay indoors. It's winter. Hide away.

But she would not succumb. She had made going out, every day, an act of self-discipline. She would visit the new exhibition at the Tate. Or go to an antique shop or two. In any case, she would bath, and dress, and tend her face. Like a soldier. There was to be no self-pity. No more fantasies.

And today, she suddenly remembered, she had arranged to take Clara to lunch. She closed her eyes and drew the deep breath her therapist had taught her. Then looked in the mirror. How I *change*, she thought crossly. How my face changes for whoever I am to meet. Look. There are the lines of disapproval appearing already, the faint hardening of my mouth. Just thinking of Clara. Already her mind racing with the responsibility: I mustn't be too well dressed; I mustn't wear a fur; I will travel by bus. Make myself push among people, become a girl again. And somehow, yes, I shall wipe off that patronizing turn from my mouth.

The only honest way to behave was to be the same with everyone. Hadn't she always believed that? Demanded

it, even, from Mendez. What a farce. She remembered
the conversation.

—Why are you so especially cruel to *me*? Do you ever
speak so angrily to anyone else? All I *ask* is a bit of
ordinary civility. Why can't you talk quietly, politely to
me, like you speak to everyone else?
—You'd like that? he'd said incredulously: Isn't it
obvious I speak more personally to you? Isn't that how
it should be? Because we're closer.
—But why should I want this constant catalogue of *your*
needs?
—Our needs, surely? What else should we discuss? Pots?
furniture?
—Anything if it could only be done peacefully, she'd
cried: Just give me the face you give everyone else. No
one would even recognize the way you look at me.
—If you prefer my public face, you shall have it, he'd
said coldly: It's not a very hopeful request. Bit remote,
to my mind.

Truly remote. Well she had her peace now certainly. Her
quiet. No more battering. No more – anything, really.
Very well. She would go upstairs to dress. Take a bath.
Choose her clothes briskly. Even thinking of it was like
fighting off a virus. She felt as if she had to *push* her
body about its tasks by a horrible act of will. Losing the
struggle. Still in her velvet wrap, she opened the door to
her sitting room. Sat. Motionless.
    Her room. Mendez' voice confirmed it.

—Your room, Lalka.
    The furniture hurt her. The textures: velvet, silk,

70

Morris wallpaper. The diversity of the curved chairs. The paintings. Chosen for Alex, though not all had pleased him. He'd like the Veuillard. But then, the whole interior clutter of round cushions, delicate-legged tables, she had made into a Veuillard. For his pleasure. Choosing the rich colours. Deep greens, golds, and many tones of violet. For him the lovely profusion of things. Their Chinese bowls, and Japanese pots with their magical gas-glaze.

And yet, perhaps he was right, perhaps it was really modelled on some old family memory; dimly from her childhood she could even see her favourite aunt's house. With Edwardian curves, and mahogany chests, and drawers; endless tiny drawers with their neat little hanging handles. Her dead aunt, who had once been an actress in the Yiddish theatre; her face even now vivid before her; slant, ironic, grey-haired, her mouth constantly flexible, changing. Her room. Yes, she *had* remembered that; buying the corner cupboard, anyway. And perhaps the rosewood table. But the rest was shared. Yes. It was their room. Their chosen room.

—In every house I've made such a room, she said aloud. Will he create one for himself in his big ugly old château?

And knew he would not. That exactly what he had once loved; and made him feel enclosed, in a great comfortable shawl of colour, now made him claustrophobic.

—Timber and stone, Tobias had said.

Hard. Cold. Bare. She would never visit the place. Never go to see it.

The tears of hatred came to her eyes as she thought of that. Tears of self-pity. Self-disgust. The desire to die.

Instead she took her first drink of the day. She knew she was going to a part of London where people would bustle and push about her; where there were open market stalls, and people selling Afghan coats, and tatty sheepskins, and bric-à-brac from Asia. That had once seemed fun to them both, she and Clara, when they were girls. And it was the past she wanted, the past; even though the traders had different faces. New hands fumbled at her wherever she went. Stall owners eyed her speculatively, and asked her to have a drink at the local pub. And these days she rebuffed them without pleasure.

So in the end, she cheated. Took a cab half across London. It was so cold.

—Put me down here, she said. And then to her astonishment saw her sister Clara across the road. She had two carrier bags, one in each hand; and was waiting for the bus. Her coat was blowing open, and the wind was sharp, but she was smiling. Waiting and smiling. Lalka hesitated. For several reasons she would have preferred not to be noticed. But she imagined the string of the two carrier bags biting into the flesh of those small plump hands, and she hesitated.

In the moment of hesitation, Clara saw her.

—What on earth are you doing in this direction? Lalka asked quickly, before Clara could ask the same thing.

—Some one's got to get the food in, Clara said: what d'you expect?

—Shops deliver.

—Not from the market they don't.

—Christ, your *lips* are going blue. I thought we arranged to have lunch.

—I haven't time, really. I phoned, said Clara: but you'd left.

—Don't be silly, Lalka insisted: We'll go somewhere round here. Why ever not?

Clara's appearance faintly irritated Lalka. Not only her appearance though, but the way her clothes brought out Lalka's own sharpness. She didn't want to be sharp, or assertive. But with the habit of years, her eyes took in Clara's flecked tweed coat, felt hat, and buttons. The giveaway fluted buttons. Lalka grimaced. Looking down the innocent, unselfconscious figure, standing so unassumingly on short legs, and small feet. Clara's shoes of course, were always elegant, because her small feet made it possible to buy good shoes from sales. But why should she choose to carry a plastic Boots handbag? With a flash of unreasonable resentment, Lalka wondered why she had never seen Clara with the good leather bag she had brought back recently from Florence.

—I'm keeping it, she explained. She *always* kept Lalka's presents. Yes, the Guerlain perfume, the ring from the Rialto.

—What the hell are you keeping them *for*? Lalka once asked aggressively.

—Occasions.

—What occasions? Your son's wedding? Lalka teased.

They went into an orange-painted, multi-arched coffee house, smelling of beefburgers and onions. Lalka said, a little queasily: Have something to eat?

—Just a coffee.

For a few moments Lalka felt her head absolutely empty. There seemed to be nothing to tell. In desperation she seized on the planned trip to Poland.

Clara stared at her in disbelief: I don't understand, she said: Why? When you could go anywhere. The Bahamas. Anywhere.

What the hell have I got to do with the Bahamas? said Lalka savagely.

—Well, I couldn't do it, said Clara. In the warmth, the colour had come back to her cheeks: All those terrible things that happened, have you no feeling? There were massacres in Kielce even after the war, you know. Peretz says.

—I don't have to listen to Peretz' lectures. Nor do you.

—He's not a fool.

—You let him lecture you, said Lalka, where's your spirit?

Clara gave her soft, sweet giggle : That's just what my son says. Edward. He's always on at me to stand up for my rights.

—And you'd like to – to please Edward? My God, does *everyone* manipulate you?

—What does it matter? I'm all right. I wouldn't care about anything if only those two got on. I just want them to be cheerful round me.

She licked her lips : That pie looks good.

—Have some, said Lalka, and do take off your hat, she begged.

The ubiquitous orange of the décor, the table mats, the formica swabbed down carelessly by a waiter from the customers before. All these things depressed Lalka profoundly. But Clara said : It's ages since I've eaten out.

She brought out a pair of glasses to read the menu. Lalka had no idea she was so short sighted. But with her black hair loose she looked prettier.

Lalka was perfectly aware that it was, in any case, not Clara's appearance that was attracting attention. The women in the café were uniformly tired-looking and drab. It was Lalka they stared at. With her lion hair and her yellow Givenchy suit, and the heavy silver and obsidian brooch at her neck.

She fidgeted.

—Did you know, said Clara : they've knocked down the old house? In Brewer Street? I went past just now and it's all rubble.

—Are we so close? Lalka was surprised.

74

—No loss to us, anyway, said Clara.

—Dad should have bought it when he had the chance. What was £300 quid? But, of course, he never believed we'd have to go on staying in such a shit-hole.

Clara's face dimpled suddenly with memory: Do you remember the outside loo? And Dad putting a dart-board on the door.

—I never used it, said Lalka. But she did remember. The hut had always frightened her, with its sweet, ambiguous smell and the blue cobwebs in the corner.

—What a mean sod he was, said Lalka: Do you remember? There was a funny green shoot came up one day out of the coal heap, and Mum used to go out and water it hopefully every day. For ages. And then it was a weed. At least *he* said it was a weed. All I know is, it was yellow.

—I don't really remember Mum, said Clara.

—Poor old girl, what a slave she was. Pinching every halfpenny. And whenever she tried to remind him about the dowry she'd brought him, he hit her. The sod.

—Lalka.

—Well, he *was* a sod, wasn't he? What did he ever do for either of us. Not that I cared. But you were the bright one, remember? *You* should have done something. You should have put up a fight.

—Do you think so? It wouldn't have made any difference.

—Yes, it would. You'd have been off out of it. At university most likely. At least you wouldn't have married Peretz.

Clara said firmly: I don't want to talk about that.

—Even now, said Lalka: it could help.

—I think I'll just have egg and chips, said Clara.

—All right. Well, I've been thinking. I tell you what – why *don't* you have a week's holiday at Easter? Nothing fancy, you can go on a package tour if you like. Just to get some sun; and have someone wait on *you* for a change. What about it? I'll have plaice, Lalka said to the waiter : if it's fresh.

—You're very generous, said Clara doubtfully : but I don't know if Peretz would let you. Pay for us.

—What? I wasn't offering to pay for him. He doesn't need a holiday. His life's one perpetual holiday.

—Being ill, said Clara : isn't a holiday. Anyway, thank you, I couldn't possibly go without him. It wouldn't be right.

—Why not, for fuck's sake? He could manage on his own for a week.

—Even if he could, said Clara doggedly : that's not the point. He'd be hurt.

Lalka was speechless.

—I couldn't just desert him like that.

Lalka said carefully : Are you so sure he's ill? Really ill? He never looks any different to me.

—Well, you don't see him often. He's ill, all right.

—His nerves, I suppose, said Lalka acidly.

—Oh, don't be so old-fashioned, said Clara angrily : that's a real disease. When he lies in bed. He just *lies* there. It's terrible to see. He doesn't even want to eat. Or live at all. All the pills round his table. Largactill 400 grams a day, he's supposed to take, but he won't. He says he doesn't want to be put out of his misery. Like a dog. But they take him off to hospital all the same, and put an electric current through his head. And then he's better.

—And begins to bully you again.

—At least he's better. He has ideas again. Starts things up. But he has such rotten luck.

—Luck, said Lalka : All right, let's go through that. First

76

there was the tobacconist at the corner. Now that had been going for twenty years before he took over.

—Before the car park came, you mean.

—Well, all right. But it still took talent to balls *that* up.

—I'm not saying he's a good business man.

—How could he be? He shouts at the customers.

—But he's had good jobs, though.

—And why does he always get the sack?

Clara flushed: He always gets to work on time; he's the hardest worker in the place. It says that. On all his testimonials.

—Then why? Lalka insisted: You know why. Don't you?

—He can't help it, Clara whispered: He does hate it so. being told what to do.

—He hates everyone, said Lalka evenly.

—No. Clara dropped her eyes.

—What about the job at the pub then?

Peretz had begun by enjoying that. The Boar's Head. He'd even come on the phone to joke to Lalka about it. Classy, it is. Little candles on the tables, and waitresses with skirts up to their bums just to take round the menus. Of course, the men do all the real cooking, and serving, and opening the bottles. Things like that.

Lalka suspected he was probably only doing a washing-up job himself but she didn't say so.

—I'm just learning the trade, he said: Maybe I'll open up on my own. In a few months.

But long before that, there was trouble. He didn't get on with the cook.

—Poor old guy, Peretz began to say: he's cowed by them all. One complaint and he's wringing his hands looking for someone to blame. And half the time the buggers only make a fuss to impress the girls they've got with them. Someone should piss in their soup.

He was an old man, the cook. Afraid for his job. His

77

wife was arthritic. Sometimes he took her home the odd partridge. He liked his position at the Boar's Head. He wasn't unkind to Peretz.

—Take one, take, he often said. At first.

Peretz came home with small birds Clara didn't know how to cook, and bottles of champagne he drank himself. Perhaps he shouldn't have accepted them. Perhaps he really *was* made into some kind of fall guy in the end, as he insisted bitterly. Perhaps he was finally rude to the manager.

Clara knew, but she wasn't likely to say. There were things she kept silent about. As Lalka had never talked about her separation from Alex. Neither sister really trusted the other.

—You put up with too much, said Lalka : You even put up with Dad.

—Well, someone had to look after him.

—Did they ?

Lalka remembered her father's features, blue-tinged with heart disease, the stiff, sharp collars biting into the tendons of his emaciated neck. The dried up, sunken face. Even the waistcoat with the gold fob watch. And the false teeth falling forward when he fell asleep to death at last in his chair. Lalka had quarrelled with him even before she was married, because he was always nagging her; trying to get her dressed in the fashion of the burghers of Krakow. My God, in London 1940. But Clara had stayed and obeyed, and baked, and tended him. And been snarled at for her pains. Even, at the end, to Peretz' fury, it was Lalka the old man left his money to; nothing for Clara. And Lalka was already rich.

—It's sad you don't remember, Mum, Lalka said softly.

—I know. Just a kind of lilac smell and softness.

—What a life you've had, Clara, said Lalka. She said it

78

without gloating. It had suddenly come over her afresh as an appalling truth, that her sister had moved from one trap to another without ever tasting independence. And yet. Independence. Wasn't that what Lalka had now? Wasn't she ill with it?

—You're *lucky* Dad died when he did, she said out loud, with sudden viciousness: or you'd still be looking after him. You'd have *three* people to give you orders. I wonder, she said reflectively: do you need someone to boss you about? Do you need that? Is it erotic?

—Lalka, please. Clara's embarrassment mounted, and her face had now flushed to the colour of an old apple: You don't understand. Not even about Peretz. He's *kind,* sometimes.

—I know. He brings you chocolates.

—At least he's loyal, said Clara: He'd never go with another woman.

—You'd be better off if he did.

Clara's thoughts had moved back to her father: Did he really yell at Mum? I only remember him at the end. His blood just turned to water, the doctor said.

—If it was ever anything else.

Lalka pulled herself up. Looking across at Clara making marks in the tablecloth with the plated fish knife, she had a sudden childhood memory. As children they had played such a strange game. *Torments.* That was it. You lay on the bed and then first one and then the other girl uncovered their delicate buttocks. Lalka could still remember breathing the deep eiderdown into her nose, and keeping her eyes tight shut, with every nerve in her tiny hairless pudenda waiting. For what? It could be anything. The surface of a brush, anything cold and surprising. Whatever it was, the touch was always disappointing. The real pleasure lay in the waiting; having one's eyes close shut. In anticipation.

79

Of course, they were too young to know that what they were waiting for was some kind of sexual assault. But they liked the game; less as they both grew towards puberty. Something half-guessed-at never occurred. Once, in exasperation though, she had hit Clara with the hairbrush quite hard, and could still hear the queer cry, that was not quite pain, before they were crying together in each other's arms. Penitent, Lalka knew now, for quite different things.

The flood of pleasure. Tears. Sex and tears.

—Christ, what a couple we are, she said : What a family to come out of.

—We were the lucky ones, said Clara, soberly.

—Because we escaped? Lalka's eyes opened : Oh no. I won't accept that. Why should we have to be grateful for that? What a bloody victory for *them*.

—Them?

—The murderers. To leave the rest of us glad just to be left to live.

Clara didn't argue the point.

—I'm tired, she said. She sounded a little forlorn.

—I'll take you back in a taxi. Shut up, I'm paying.

—No. I can't. Peretz is at home.

—Well, he shouldn't be.

—If you want to know, said Clara : he's starting up on his own again.

—And where did he get the money? This time.

—I gave it him.

—How? Or do you mean I did? said Lalka.

—No. I earnt it. I've been working, said Clara, and she pushed back her hair which had fallen over her eyes, with a little flick of pride : Working in a shop. On commission. I made a lot last week.

—My God, you aren't a woman, you're a *horse*, said Lalka : You'll drop dead. Stupid. Stubborn. Horses run

80

themselves to death for men, did you know that?

—But I'm fine, cried Clara: I'm doing it for Edward. I want to.

And indeed she looked remarkably well. A little less plump, perhaps, but that suited her; the even seed-shaped teeth unimpaired. There was no sourness in her.

When she had gone Lalka found the flabby chips had given her a pain in the gut.

The phone was going as Lalka arrived home. It was Katie.

—Darling, I'm sorry. Bad news. That cunt Trevor, she said: called me two minutes ago. We're a bit *pushed* this month, sweetie, he says to me. We'll have to re-think. Well, I know what that means.

Lalka unbuttoned her coat with one hand, and tried to support the phone between her ear and her shoulder: I can't hear you. It's so cold today. Is it serious?

—What? Don't be so bloody naive, Lalka. Don't you recognize a put-down when you hear one. He'd like me back on the woman's page. That's what it is. And he thinks he can scare me out of pushing the Polish trip.

—Well, Poland *is* very cold just now, really sub-zero cold, perhaps, after all.

—Oh, that's all knickers. I've dished him. Listen, I went over his head. Completely. To Norman.

—Was that right?

Katie paused: How do you mean right? Anyway, it worked. It's not a hundred per cent even now, I admit. But if you still want to come.

—I suppose I do.

—Thank you very much. What's changed?

—Nothing, said Lalka, bleakly.

—You can tell me.

—No, I cannot, said Lalka, firmly.

And certainly she could not. She was already ashamed herself of her own childish reasoning. What? Suprise a man who wasn't even there to care? My God, would even *dying* do that? She had no desire to hear Katie's knowing guffaw. So she concluded lamely : Perhaps I'm getting 'flu.

—Then have a rum. Go to bed. Don't go out. Did you know the bug is absolutely *deadly* this year? See your doctor, there's a vaccine.

—I'm not creeping about yet, said Lalka.

—Well, at least get the vaccine.

—Will you stop bullying me? Lalka flashed.

Katie paused : My dear, you sound most peculiar. I'm sure you're not telling me something.

—I'm not telling you anything, said Lalka : goodbye.

In February the weather changed. A false spring filled London with uneasy radiance. Cold blue skies over painted barges and bridges; wet pavements glowing. Yellow light everywhere. Even the grey walls of Lalka's town garden turned yellow. The twigs of the bare trees had an aureole of sunlight like golden smoke in their branches. Lalka watched through her windows. She was behind glass again, her resolutions oddly failing her in the warm air.

It was spring, and nothing had happened as she'd hoped. Tobias had visited Mendez and he was fine. Absolutely fine, she knew that. Only he hadn't bothered to write or call. Hadn't bothered.

Katie had found a new man. She was walking in the garden of Eden. Everything was changed for her; she was every dead thing in which love wrought new alchemy, she said. And didn't phone for days at a time.

Lalka phoned once herself; and put down the receiver quickly when the new voice answered. Of all people it was Trevor. For years the arch-enemy. Lalka couldn't bring herself to cope with such extraordinary changes in feeling. She wondered if Katie's husband had moved out.

She caught herself envying Clara the opportunity of being a simple, loyal wife. It was all she was good for herself, she decided unhappily, because the desire for other men somehow failed to awaken. It wouldn't bother her if she never touched the naked body of another man again. Even Mendez she no longer dreamed of sexually. When she thought of him it was with sadness only. Even the persistent voice in her head made itself heard less angrily. She thought of walking through New York at his side, at the sense of safety his size had always given her. All her resentments vanished in memories of his gentleness, his patient battle with her over the years. When she thought of that she wanted to weep. Sometimes she did, and Maria brought her a bottle of valium now with her poached eggs in the morning. Many days she ate almost nothing.

Towards the end of February she woke to a burst of bird song, out of a dream of such happiness, that for a moment she could not remember where she was. She had been in Italy, and for a moment she looked up expecting to see Fiesole out of her window. Before she had quite returned to herself, the telephone rang at her bedside. She picked it up, pushing away her hair, and answered with a light voice.

At the other end of the line was a quiet, almost forgotten voice.
—Alex.

She was so filled with joy that she could hardly grasp what he said. The line crackled. He was ringing from Aix, he must be. Far away. And yet the cadences of the voice in her ear were so familiar, so continuous with her dream that she looked around the lit room as if it had been flown southward to be close to him.

It was some time before she grasped the words.

—A *child*?

Even when she heard what he said, she could not grasp the import of it. The morning light faded from her thought; she could no longer hear the birds. Her voice grew breathy, not with hysteria, not even panic, but as though her rib-cage had begun to function unreliably. Her throat tightened and hurt.

—Hello?

—Yes. I did hear you.

—The line is so bad.

—I can hear you. Yes.

—Perhaps I should have written.

—Do you want to marry the girl? She brought out. She was suddenly conscious that her heart was banging loudly in her chest. She wondered foolishly if he could hear it.

—Not necessarily. How are you placed?

She could not answer him.

—I suppose you must mind. A little.

—No. Why should I mind? she said tonelessly: Congratulations.

—Thank you.

Mind? After all their long, childless years, after all those ignominious test, visits to specialists, expensive weeks in clinics in the States. Why should she mind?

It was only at the end of the conversation that he said casually; as if going east, back to Poland, were the most ordinary thing in the world; as if Lalka had *always* set out on holidays alone; as if there were simply *nothing* to it : Have a good trip. If you contact me before you go, I'll explain the system of changing *zloty* to you. Or you'll be hopelessly diddled. Don't change money in the street, he warned her, it isn't necessary.

—Yes, Alex, she said meekly : yes. I'll get in touch again before I go.

She couldn't bring herself to say *we*. Not while Katie's new love-affair lasted. There *was* no we. Only one person who was transformed and transfigured by love, and another who was being gradually swept out and out like a piece of floating weed in the tide of the sea. Out and further out from any kind of hold or firm land.

Later in the day, still in bed, she suddenly remembered. How could she have forgotten? The last gynaecologist had been absolutely positive. Even jocular.

—Mrs Mendez, you could have a hundred babies. There are no problems. Nothing is wrong with you.

—Then, why, why, why?

—Your husband.

—That can't be possible.

—Why not? Because he is good in bed? Luckily the two things don't go together.

—But all his family. They all had so many children.

—Mrs Mendez, if you think about it, such a difficulty could hardly be hereditary.

She was silenced.

—In any case, the tests are very simple. Send Mr Mendez to see me, and we can find out which of the many possibilities is the problem. You know, in so many cases, these days, something can be done.

—He will never believe me.

—Simply send him to see me.

—No.

Why not? She couldn't have explained. How it was in some way perfectly aesthetic for the fault to be hers; he was used to it; the thought didn't appal him. So they could continue. But to think of his sperm failing? He would not like that. Irrationally, she was certain the news would be deadly. To her.

—No, she repeated : I insist.

And she sat and marvelled. What luck, she thought. The gynaecologist had been wrong all the time. It would *all* have come out; and it was *she*, and *she* alone, who would have been blamed.

If the gynaecologist was wrong.

She pinched her ear reflectively. Then a small, malicious grin began to form itself on her lips uncertainly. Her blood danced. She was almost ashamed at her thought.

If.

Suddenly Lalka felt an enormous desire for food. A large steak, piled over with mushrooms. Some *petits pois.* She buzzed Maria. And when she looked in her dressing-table mirror she seemed to have lost ten years.

7

—It's not as though you want me here. Not with you, I mean, said Lee fretfully : You just can't *keep* me here feeding me yoghurt and steaks, and spend all your time in that spooky old library.

—But why do you want to go to Aix? asked Mendez, mildly.

Lee went on brushing her long hair. There was something childlike in her thoroughness. Her mouth was shut, as if she might be counting the strokes of her arm. Her strangeness now seemed to him rather like the uncertainty of a half-tamed animal; needing protection and still likely to bite. Yes. A girl in bare feet taking bread from her lover's hand.

—Suppose I just want to go out and see some kids of my own age?

—You can still be driven there in the car.

—Spy.

—That's unfair, protested Mendez.

She turned from the mirror and stared at him.

—I'm just a sort of vessel for *it*, aren't I, Alex? That's why you're suddenly so bloody protective.

—No. Mendez felt a flash of irritation. He would have liked to shake her; to *make* her get it right. And yet it *was* true, too, that he feared for the child, the son he already felt in her.

—I don't even want a child, she'd said at first, sullenly :
I can't see why *you* do. Now. And, my God, why this
one?

—Well, I do. It needn't tie you. You can leave him with
me afterwards if you want to travel. What's the problem?

—You treat me like a breeding cow, she said : That's
what.

But there was something else bothering her, frightening
her, he knew. He waited patiently for it to come out. She
went round obliquely.

—I'm too old, she said : I'm over thirty. The child will be
mongoloid, or else I'll have to be cut open. I don't want
to go *through* all that.

—You're talking nonsense. My mother had her last child
in her forties. Are you over *thirty*? How much over? If.

—Your mother had nine children first. For all I know
she dropped her children in a field. Well, I'm not *strong,*
Alex.

—Look, the gynaecologist says . . .

—The gynaecologist, the gynaecologist. He'll get his fee
anyway, won't he? He isn't knocking years off *his* life, is
he? Why should he care? You must be the last man in
the world to believe in the medical profession.

—I told him you were scared.

—Look. My hips are too small. I'm not a great robust
madam like my mother. Or your wife, if it comes to that.
I'll split open.

—Lee, it's the pelvis, not the hips. Honestly, there's no
danger.

She thinned her lips : All right. Supposing I just don't
want it? What if I just have my own reasons why not?
I can still go away you know, even you can't stop me.

And at first he was afraid of that. Because he sensed
there was some buried fear she was still hiding. Later he
was even afraid she'd harm the child deliberately. Now

his fears swarmed only about her welfare. He thought how easily she might accidentally damage the child through boredom, smoking hash, or just the habit of self-neglect. Her driving terrified him. And once she realized that she'd taunted him with the fear.

—How about if I smash myself up in the car? What'd happens to your bloody child then?

—You speak like a fool, he'd said coldly.

Today the wind blew hard through the stunted olive trees. Mendez could hear its moan through the two layers of glass. He could see the ferocity of the northern air pulling and shaking everything alive in the grey limestone cliffs. A wild, vicious wind. The eroded earth blew about in it; the dryness made his throat ache. Meanwhile, Lee had turned away from him. She was pressed close up to the glass.

In February, in Menton, walking between the great beds of lemons, oranges, and avocados; all the wired fruit decorations; with Lee at his side he had felt her gaiety as intoxicating as the scent of citrus skins. Now he knew her spirit was as bitter as any of the oranges grown on some deformed hybrid trees.

And then he saw she had been scratching on the glass with a diamond he had given her. While he meandered in thought. He could read the words clearly:

Au ciel. Resistez.

—Very appropriate, said Mendez: Thank you. So you see yourself as Marie Durand of Château d'If, do you? Wasn't she locked up for thirty years? From a very young child?

—Yes, said Lee.

—You speak like a child, certainly said Mendez. Otherwise . . .

—I was seven when I left this place, she said: I never wanted to return. It was only your bloody servant got me here. Ugh. I can still taste everything. As it was. You may have torn out the plaster, or the wood, Alex, but you haven't got rid of the smell.

—Of what?

—My ghosts. They're all still here.

Mendez sat down.

—Tell me about your ghosts.

—Roomfuls. Crouched in the old cupboards, with the meters and the pipes ticking. Old men with lice in their beards. And shit-stained children. Women as old as witches.

—Refugees.

—Yes. God, why are they so ugly, refugees? So ugly and smelly and so pathetically without dignity? Grateful. For anything – water, bits of bread.

—Yes, said Mendez.

—Even the children. So bony and dumb. They hardly spoke. Mendez said neutrally: I wonder how many of them got away. You are a long way from the coast here.

—At first it was the French, not the Germans, my mother had to look out for. She knew them, how to deal with them.

—Surely by 1943, said Mendez: it must have been too late? And they would have had no money.

—No. They weren't all poor. They had rings. Diamonds.

She flushed.

Mendez saw thin arms at gratings, cries from closed trains; splinter chips of loved rings.

—But where could they hope to go? he inquired.

—Tunisia, perhaps. Even Italy. I don't know. When the German soldiers came, the officers were very polite. They arranged for helpers. To clean up. And snoop. My mother – she behaved like their natural ally. But still they sent in old village crones. With faces like dried figs. To spy on us. Oh, of course they spied. You could see it in their gummy eyes. What else did they do? There was still soot, grease, dirt everywhere.

—And the refugees?

—We had to board them in. They didn't understand. They wouldn't stop. Slobbering, whimpering. And . . . Above their new cupboards, you know, we had the women: sanding, and drying, and waxing the floor.

—For the ballroom?

—Yes, for the Germans to move in.

She laughed.

—They were clean and blue-eyed and handsome, the officers. My mother entertained them. Do you think I didn't know? That I didn't see? How well she did it?

—Were you jealous? said Mendez gently.

—Then, one day, the Germans broke through the sealed doors. They pulled the nails out of the crossed boards and found the window-frames. After that . . .

She fell silent.

—Suppose I told you, she said: that it wasn't the village women, whatever they knew. That – I was the one who betrayed her? Whispered the secret. To one of *them*.

—I should say, you were too young to remember. That it was just fantasy.

—After that, I don't know. I didn't see. I was hiding under my bed. I held my coral crucifix.

He soothed her, but she shook off his hands.

—You think I care what happened to your Jews, don't you? That's not even part of it – I hated them Alex, don't you understand. I *hated* them.

—You were only a child.

—I don't even care now. I don't *care* what happened to them. Good God, anyone can fall out of the sky, or be shot in the street, or just drop dead at forty with a heart attack. That's what life's *like*. It's *not* safe, keep the rules, move straight round the board. Not for anyone. What's so special about *that* lot dying? Half the world lives in rags, starves. It can't be that, either.

—Then why are you haunted? He asked.

She stood there before him, sucking her wrist, her narrow shoulders looking too weak to support a child : a child herself. Then she said, abruptly : I'm afraid here. Can I go out now?

Mendez said : Very well. Take whichever car you like. Be careful.

—I'll be late, she said : Poor Alex. Go back to your books. Isn't that what you came here for? Not to have me. You wanted to read and think and understand, didn't you? Wasn't that it? Now's your chance.

She gave him a quick skip of a kiss. Sighed : I wish you weren't so bloody indulgent. Well. At least I want you to remember I didn't *pretend*.

And from the great baroque arches of his library windows he watched her leave. He didn't believe the story of her own guilt. Or rather. What she said only made her seem even more vulnerable to him. He wanted to hover like an invisible protector over her. Not to spy. Not to know. Only to look after her. To keep her safe.

And he smiled. He was not afraid of her ghosts. Those poor tired fugitives, let them rest, he would not call them. Perhaps one day he might sow grass for them in one corner of the lowest field, where the water ran. No stones, there were enough abandoned stones already. Lee was guiltless. Wasn't she? As he was. All they had done was to walk a bad road a little earlier, to have been a little luckier, never to have hidden, or been forgotten in a cupboard. It was no more than chance. And yet. Remorsefully, he recalled how he had felt so much more blame for Lalka. And her refusals to remember. All that had happened. Why, he wondered, had he demanded so *much* more from her? Over so many years. If he were to settle now for the loveliness of a haunted child, who probably already smelt in his own flesh the sick pallor of the people she had feared and resented.

Mendez returned to his books. He had been reading about the Hassidic seer, the Baal Shem Tov. Tonight he found a letter from the Baal Shem Tov to his brother-in-law. Was it only Jews, though Mendez, who had saints with brothers-in-law? The letter reported a conversation with the Angel of Death. Why, the Baal Shem had asked, do you massacre so many innocent Jews?

And what reply did he get?

—I do it for the sake of heaven, for the love of God and for his glory.

A macabre evasion, but the real question was: why was Mendez reading about men of God at all? What God? After Birkenau, Treblinka, Dachau. Was he seriously casting about in the black unbreathable unimaginable nothingness round the planet for some long-bearded? No. He understood very well that it was only Man, most vicious of all gods, who ruled. But then . . . That was the disaster he was looking back into.

Tobias had once observed with surprise, and some incredulity: I notice you feel some affection for the Germans? After everything.

—Why should I hate them? Fool. You think of what happened as a *national* crime. How simple. I don't care *which* nation threw living children into the fires; only that *men* find it easy to do these things. That is what is terrifying.

All of which a few lunatic, melancholic seers, followers of the first Hassid had prefigured. So he read them. Or about them.

Not that what they offered was much help or guidance. As they knew. In one story a certain Reb Wolf, at the moment of death, spoke to his servant as follows: I can see a day will come, and it fills me with fear. The world will lose all stability, and man all reason. Tell the people on that day none will be spared, not even the most virtuous, no one.

At which news the servant asked: When that day comes, what must they do?

—When that day comes, tell our people that I have foreseen it. At which point the Hassid turned his face to the wall and died.

So much for prophecy. How well they knew its weakness. And yet sometimes their tales had the resonance of something darker. It was said of Zusia and his brother that they arrived one night in a small village near Krakow; but were so pursued by restlessness they had to leave before morning. It is a village the Poles called Oswiecim; and later the Germans were to name it Auschwitz.

There were men who feared terror less than the heart of the next generation. That it would grow arid, that the souls of mankind would become ugly. In such fantasy, a beadle hung himself from the carved brass chandelier in the synagogue; and another melancholy man was so haunted by the sadness of his phantom that he collapsed in Tanner Street in what must, Mendez supposed, have been a state of acute melancholia.

All was joy and song when they danced; about them the poor tallow-makers, and small-piece merchants, leather craftsmen, and tool-makers alike, danced in their prayer shawls for the glory of God. Yet how many of their seers, Mendez tried to count, attempted suicide?

Occasionally he came across a saying that filled him with anger. 'Whoever chooses solitude, chooses death.' Fair enough. But the reason? 'If you look only into your own soul, you are bound to despair; but if you look outside at creation you are bound to be filled with joy.'

What innocence! As if outside was nothing but turning seasons, and vegetable grace at appointed times, as if there were no deserts and dead seas. And supposing you looked out on a square where men hung garrotted; what joy then? In meekness, resignation, gentle acceptance?

The meek. Yes. The meek inherit the earth. That was true. The gentle in spirit. Shall inherit. Soil, clay soil, and their bones shall be covered with bones, other men's bones, and the spades of their enemies, shall level ditches over them, unclothed in the earth. The earth, which is the end of miracles, the end of the songs and legends, the final song and legend. In fields of uncollected hair and long-rotten shoes, the earth still lies which was that inheritance. For those who danced in the cattle trucks towards Birkenau; and those who went the same rails to the same trenches, the same limepit. In bewilderment. To the same impartial God, and the same earth. Waiting.

Mendez shook his head. Lifted his eyes. In that case why did he want a child? Why did he feel happy at the thought, as if it could be in some sense a victory; a piece of human flesh won from intended darkness?

He admitted it to himself. Against all the evidence, he still believed in the human. He was ashamed. He could not acquit himself. What he read was after all his tradition also; even after all he knew. Even, he supposed, after all the dark story tellers had seen. For whatever reason.

In power-cut London. Insomniac. Sluggish. Ill. Tobias pored over the sharp beam that lit his neat desk. Usually he liked to work at night. But tonight he could do nothing. He got up. Paced about. The olive drab room constricted him. He threw open the curtains, to rid himself of the heavy dull silence, the sleazy taste of his own night breathing. But outside the darkness of the streets was terrifying; the silence flowed in from there in waves. He clutched at familiar objects; the trees, black and spread wide in the centre of his square; but their branches were dark. And the quietness was dark also. He could hear nothing but a single man tapping along with his umbrella used as a stick. The parked cars were silent as the objects in a dream.

Tobias looked down at his hands. They were strong and white, and his nails were fine. But his palms were wet. He was soaked to the bone as if he were running a fever. Even his own grey velvet armchairs appalled him; his old squat Chesterfield appeared to sit before him with something too decisive a solidity. Sick night spooks. He was not used to them. Or so many layers of thought, surfacing one after another. Above all, he was used to keeping his mind linear; he liked to think in syntax.

He clenched his hands. Took up a pen. Began to write a letter he knew he would never send. Just to keep his thoughts in order, in sequence. To keep himself sane.

My dear Alex,

I find myself in some moral perplexity. Not to be obscure : I have for my own purposes spent a good deal of energy collecting a body of information together which, I have to say, primarily concerns you. I'm sure you don't want it, won't like it, and will probably choose to ignore it. I'm not sure I ought for any of those reasons to keep it from you.

Bluntly then. I have been investigating both Miss Walsh and her burglar boy-friend. Contain your anger. As the lawyer who obtained her release, the initial involvement was automatic. Files were put at my disposal. Whatever you might have preferred, I have to admit I was then incapable of leaving matters as they stood.

Jack Lacey, then, is the name of the young man who has been Miss Walsh's constant companion for the last two years. His political alignment is unsurprising; he has been attached to a militant down-with-parliament leftist group ever since he completed his studies at the Free University of Berlin a few years ago. No doubt you will dismiss *that* as harmless youthful idealism. The English police do not : but I imagine you will shrug that aside equally, since you usually take the conventional liberal stand on such questions. I have to say I also think he is decidedly dangerous; but then, to your mind, I'm hopelessly craven, so I don't expect that opinion to carry any weight with you. In any event, craven or not, I have taken the trouble to meet and talk with the boy. He is a spoilt rich brat, from a family that supported Mosley in the thirties; nominally in hippy flight and revolt from his background, but still driving a yellow Alfa Romeo. He hates all the pantheon of capitalist villains; of which I'm afraid (ironic as you may find it) you are one; and very cheerfully contemplates their physical destruction. He is a member of no English political group, because, he says, none of them are sufficiently extreme.

All of which continues to concern you, my dear Alex, because, as he freely admits, he has been regularly meeting Miss Walsh for the last few months in which she has been living in your château.

Tobias stopped writing. Because the images which then forced themselves upon him were not so easily expressed with precision. And how could he admit to

Mendez an old pathology; the seduction he felt himself
for the boy's cold eyes and the severity of his hatred of
flab; the immediate flow of understanding between
them. How he understood the boy, when he said he
would have preferred the vilest brute for an ancestor
than a string of tender, yellow victims.

They had sat in the low car waiting behind a bus for
some time, and through Tobias' open window came the
rotten, sweet smell of fruit in the gutters, fallen from
market stalls. All around them were the noises of engines
ticking over, a heavy lorry, an old Renault, a Morris
Minor.

And the yellow car could only crawl two feet and then
stop. Tobias watched Lacey becoming bored and irrit-
able. Saw him yawn and lean on his elbow, watching
the woman at her fruit stall. She was fat, with gingery
hair growing grey; her face blank, apart from two lines
which ran down from her nose. Her hands were white
and podgy. When she bent down to find something under
the stall, her bottom pushed out her shiny black coat like
the haunch of a cow.

Then she began to cross the road, stepping between
the nose of the yellow car and the bus ahead. Still leaning
back, Lacey pressed his foot across the accelerator with
his toe. The car roared and jerked against the clutch.
The woman gave a sudden jump forward, and then
seeing the other lane of traffic begin to move, looked
wildly into the windscreen into Lacey's eyes. Lacey met
her frightened stare with his bluest, blankest indifference.

Oh yes, I know him well; mused Tobias. He is one of
those who would always rejoice to see heads roll, and
bellies explode. He would laugh, because he had some
sickness of revenge in his heart. And because what he
hated was so absolute, so much part of the human : all
softness. Which Tobias also hated. Yes, he recognized the

98

same chill in them both; in imagination he could taste it on the boy's narrow lips. An old taste that took him back to schooldays and the almost forgotten, buried, denied, lusts of his boyhood.

Against his will he remembered love. For another cool, blue-eyed aristocrat, who had treated him with contempt. Dead drunk now. Or even dead. But Tobias could still hear the absurdly confident lift in that young voice, and the way his sentences rose, in a surprised drawl, that stopped just short of a sneer.

—Urbane? I was urbane in the cradle.

At Oxford, Tobias had been under his thrall. Gawky under amused blue eyes, that could outstare any disaster, and reduce it to delight. At his best in slapstick situations. Loving to be outside the law, and take Tobias out of it. With gibes and prods, every weapon of verbal contempt.

Once Tobias had bought a mahogany table for his room, and his friend had become suspicious of the quality of the wood. Nothing would satisfy him but an instant inspection at 2 a.m. of the genuine Georgian tables owned by the college.

The dining room was open. They entered easily. Neatly, as Tobias watched, the brass hooks of the long table were unhooked by knowing hands; smoothly a penknife took a neat shaving of wood from the hidden edge. Tobias begged him to be satisfied with one sample. He was downed with a reproachful glare.

—We'll be caught, Tobias found himself saying.

And his friend's eyebrows flew upward as Lacey's had, in amusement, as Lacey's face had confronted the frightened lady nearly under the powerful grille of his car.

And soon another table was prised gently open, and another small sliver of wood removed with a delicate knife.

—Pinkish, you see?

—That's enough. Absolutely. I see what you mean.

It had been enjoyable for ten minutes. Crossing the court, they were comrades. And then suddenly, in the darkness of the staircase up to Tobias' rooms, his friend attacked him. Viciously. Not playfully. Not because they were drunk. But out of a stronger boy's almost erotic need to break the complicity of laughter and re-establish supremacy. Tobias had fought craftily with his arms at first, breaking his friend's wrestling holds, rolling himself out from under the heavy punches. Until at last. At the bottom of the stairs they had both fallen together in a heap on a broken bottle.

And with the sound of the breaking glass, the mood of both had changed. For the first time, Tobias saw the temptation of violence in his friend's face. He was not afraid. He was cold. He lunged for the neck of the glass. Missed. Sprawled.

And watched his friend's face dissolve into laughter.

In his fall he had become a victim.

Without triumph, and almost carelessly, the elder boy lifted the jagged edge of the bottle and scored a jagged cut across the back of Tobias' hand.

The blood released them both. Tobias felt no pain. He lay without anxiety, watching the red liquid soaking into his neat cuffs; waiting. Unafraid.

—Fool, he said. Without moving.

—Is it deep?

—How can I tell in this light?

It was deep enough. Tobias still carried the white line of it ten years later on the back of his hand. But the incident had not affected his attachment. Later in that term Tobias had slept with his friend's marvellous French mistress; could hardly wait afterwards to tell him of the betrayal. But the other only said: Why ever not? Everyone else has. He was untouchable.

Tobias knew Lacey. As Mendez never could, because he had no understandings of the springs of spite; the chill pleasures of it. Black as the tide of darkness that rushed in at Tobias from the London street outside.

Lacey could do anything.

And still Tobias crumpled up his warning letter. And threw it, soberly, into his wicker basket.

Could Mendez know if the child Lee carried was his? Tobias did not believe any words of his could avert what must be coming.

As to Miss Walsh. As to Lee. Her beauty had made Tobias into Lacey's agent. Against his knowledge, and altogether his own intentions and desires, for which lack of calculaton Tobias could not forgive himself. Malice and envy he understood; but stupidity made him ashamed. And so, yes, he had brought himself to go back even to Oliver Walsh and make enquiries. But there was nothing. No asylums, no schizophrenic record, no medical history. Though Oliver nodded vehement agreement at every suggestion of disorder. But for that strange amnesiac expression, which turned her features so unexpectedly from those of a grown woman into those of a lost child, Oliver had no explanation whatsoever.

Mendez woke in his library, just before morning, to the sound of loud music. For a moment, it seemed to him that he still was in the grip of a dream, the music seemed to vibrate so strongly in the air about him. But as he shook off his doziness he understood that no guitars made so much noise without electronic amplification. He picked out a flute. And a voice. Lee's voice. Perhaps even Lee's voice would need a microphone to reach down the long stone corridors and wake him here. He listened to the pure rising exhilaration in her voice for a moment with lonely pleasure. When she sang, Lee's voice had all the confidence her fragile body lacked. But then he frowned to think she had been up all night, and was even now driving herself into deeper fatigue.

A little anxiously, he stretched and rose, to go and collect her; and it was only then he wondered who exactly she had brought in through his fortress walls. Without invitation. A little sleepily, he stacked his books. He decided that it was unreasonable to object. Never the-less. In bare feet, tying his silk belt, and still lulled by the sweet rising notes, he moved off purposefully to end the party.

8

—Oh, that's all over. I blew it, said Katie.

—Well, good.

—I don't know about good, what's good?

Quietly and gently the Essex landscape flattened out into the brown water of the harbour, making no shoreline; grass and hedgerows trailed out straight into the sea, Harwich itself out of sight. It was almost as if the huge boat, rising and falling, had been moored in a field. As if England itself were just such a softly curving mound of peacefulness.

—You're resilient, that's good.

—*Am* I, though? What do you make of it, Lalka? I've been in the most awful misery for days.

Katie stood up restlessly, her new dress billowing about her so that she seemed to float in it; glowing with physical strength.

—Shall we go and eat? Before the seats all go.

—I'm not very hungry, said Lalka, standing up nevertheless.

The last time I saw you, said Katie suspiciously: you looked absolutely bloody marvellous. What's up?

—Well, we're off aren't we?

—Is that what's wrong?

—Not *wrong* exactly.

—For Godsake, are you still mooning about after Mendez?

—It's nothing to do with a man. I don't think I'm very

interested in who I sleep with at the moment. Or even if.

Lalka did not feel ill; but she knew her face and voice had the sag of energy failure in them. She hoped it was only hormonal; reversible at least. But it had begun weeks earlier; with the first creeping of a gelatinous protective ooze over her responses, a sort of psychological lymph, released to seal away as much as possible of her inner life from her knowledge. But now she was so white and blank inside, she could only just make out the faint outlines of familiar regrets and desires. Her thoughts had solidified. It was as if nothing any longer moved freely inside her.

Katie found the last table near a port-hole two minutes ahead of an impudent, good-looking young Irishman, who yielded at once to her stare, and sat himself courteously at the next table.

Together they studied the menu.

—My God, how tatty it all is, groaned Katie.

The waiter, who was already at Lalka's elbow flinched visibly. Lalka felt the flinch in her own flesh, and tried to mollify him with a smile. But his attention was fixed on Katie.

—Let's try the soup, she suggested.

—2 soup, he scribbled eargerly: Soup of the day or tomato?

—What is soup of the day?

He consulted the card at the back. Paused. Clearly Katie had made him nervous.

—Well. Tomato, he admitted.

Katie laughed: All right, that's easy.

He bustled off, anxious to please. At the next table the young Irishman tried to catch Katie's eye, and smiled. But she had already leapt up out of her place. The boat had begun to leave the dockside, and she wanted to watch it pass the headland. She was up and out of the glass doors, while Lalka continued to sit mutely.

The pale orange soup arrived. The waiter was at her elbow. He had obviously hurried to please, and now a high flush of bewilderment rose under the bloom of his skin. He was stung with the pain of the soup growing cold. He hovered. He wondered if he should take the liquid away. Lalka felt her own nerves torn with the responsibility of reassuring him.

—Quite extraordinary, said Katie returning : You should have come. For Godsake what are you goggling at?

This time the Irishman succeeded in catching her eye, and Katie giggled companionably back at him. Lalka tried to focus on the menu, but her gorge rose at the smell of food. She tried to explain about the waiter.

They had to wait longer for cutlets. Perhaps the waiter had been timing it deliberately. And still, even as the meat arrived, Katie was up again before he brought the vegetables. She wanted to see the new derricks being built on the marshes, she said. And there the poor man was again with his neat little silver-plate dishes. Like a worried child, he bothered Lalka pathetically. Should he take away the plates? Heat them up? What?

—Can't you see you're driving the man mad, she whispered to Katie as she returned.

—Really? Katie stared around, trying to recognize the man among the other white-coated bustling figures : Which is he? The bald one? With no eyebrows? Perhaps he's on the edge of the loony bin anyway.

—No need to push him over.

—How absurd. Next time I'll leave him a reassuring note. Not offended, gone to pee. Something like that.

Lalka tried to pick up Katie's laconic manner and failed. There was something in the waiter's whole demeanour; even his description of the menu (evasive, and yet eager to please) that stirred some uneasy buried recognition. And he was having trouble with the table on the other side too. She could hear the servility in his voice.

—*Not* two duck? I'm sorry.

Every bent head and raised eyebrow drew his anguished regard. Through the glass doors, like a silent screen comic he came, bowing and nodding, and nearly mad with the pressure on him.

Surreptitiously, Lalka left him an absurdly generous tip.

—Can I join you?

They moved to take their coffee in the blue leatherette comfort of the coffee lounge. Katie looked up, surprised. it was the young Irishman. Lalka dropped her eyes uncomfortably. He was a little drunk, not very; but he carried a full glass of brandy in his hand and his eyes on Katie were distinctly speculative.

—Let me buy you both a drink, he urged.

They all drank brandy. The effect on Lalka was to move her one stage further into her own remote whiteness. She was at a remove. She wasn't listening. She was astonished when he suddenly turned to her and said: And what are *your* troops doing in Ireland?

—My?

—That's right. Look at her, he said to Katie: I mean in America at least by now *you'd* have a protest movement. Twenty thousand troops. Been there two years. And *she* doesn't even know why. Tell me. Do you?

—I didn't, she began.

—Look at her, honest to God, it's terrifying. She doesn't know.

—I don't, said Lalka.

106

—It's bloody terrifying. Supposed to be intellectuals, aren't you? Read all the papers anyway. Just don't care enough to find out. *Do* you read? Did you read today those kids were killed?

—I think you're having too much of that brandy, said Katie : This is a five-hour trip, take it easy.

—I'm not going away till she answers.

—Well, said Lalka weakly : I suppose by now most people would like to pull the troops out. I would.

—So *they* shouldn't get hurt, I suppose? Poor bleeders. Much it matters to you what they've done. An occupying power, that's what you are.

—Christ, said Lalka, in sudden fury : that's a nerve.

—Aha.

—D'you hear? Lalka felt her voice strengthen : Don't talk to me about occupations.

She stood up.

—Can we go? she said to Katie.

—That's right. Run away from the truth. That's the English all over.

—English? I'm *not* English, said Lalka with a sudden surge of power : And I haven't run away across half Europe to have some drunken oaf lecture *me* about persecution.

—Quietly, said Katie : people are looking.

—Let them, Lalka's mind was swimming.

The broad, honest face before her was blank with surprise at her outburst. But she couldn't stop. She was angry. And for the first time for weeks she remembered where she was going. Her mind changed colour. It was red. The blood beat in it.

—My troops, she said : I never had any troops to protect me. Shall we exchange dead? Murdered children? Families?

—Listen, said Katie : I think we'll go up to the top deck.

107

The Irishman made a friendly gesture to Katie, tapping his forehead with a finger sympathetically: Bleeding hysteric, he said.

As they went up the stairs, Lalka could feel her knees shaking. It was not fear, she recognized; it was excitement. She had enjoyed the encounter. She felt much better. She was sure the colour had come back to her cheeks, as the blood had run back to her brain.

But Katie watched her queerly.

—Sit down, she said : Just sit quietly, I've some work to do.

And went on scribbling in her blue notebook, while Lalka lit a cigarette. Her right hand began to shake. She watched it with surprise.

—Now what's all this not English nonsense? said Katie, I'd leave that off where we're going.

—I don't know, said Lalka, frightened : I never thought it before. I've always felt. Grateful. Rather humble about it.

Meek. Always one of the meek. Like Clara, even. English, of *course*. What else? I've lost my way she thought. Why? Had she ever allowed herself to be talked into this absurd journey. What was the point of going back; down; to poke about among the worms; the lost; what good could come of it? And worst of all, she thought, I have thrown away the only man who would have wanted to share this experience with me. Once. It's too late now. Her heart was squeezed with the pain of that.

—Lalka, you must do things for yourself now.

It was weeks since her head had recalled Alex' voice.

For herself. Well, but then who *was* she, this Lalka? Who should she be? And why should she want so hungrily to find out? It would be the first time she had made such a demand on herself. She supposed it was because, suddenly, she seemed to have so little to lose, she could risk anything; expose herself to any experience. Without fear. She was even eager for. Anything. That would bring her to life. To know herself. To *become* herself. Even if that self was an unhappy stranger in a hostile world.

She looked across at Katie. As she sat, biting her pencil. Scribbling. Her radiant green eyes. Blue green. Like the eyes in the tail of a peacock. Broad face. Square teeth.

—Women, said Katie looking up; I say, Lalka, did you ever have a flirtation with a Lesbian?

—No, my God, said Lalka. Perhaps a shade too quickly.

—Only woman I ever fell for, said Katie: Went seven weeks start to finish. Flop. I sometimes wonder if it ever happened.

—What did? Happen?

—Well, she had this marvellous eighteenth-century cottage, with real Bacon paintings on the walls. Move in, she said. You can just knock on the wall, that's how it'll be. Come and live here. We'll go on having men, but it won't matter, we'll not depend on them; soon as one of us feels freaky we'll just knock on the wall, like that. Come in. Have a drink. It'll be great. And I felt so low then. Well. At first we phoned each other every day. But I never did move in. She just cooled off the idea. Just like a fucking *man*.

—Were you unhappy?

—I think I was for a bit. I suppose I'd got used to the idea she really thought I was great.

—So that's why you call it a love-affair?

—Well, that's what they're like mostly.

—Not for me.

—Well, it's different for you. You don't have to get

bolstered, do you? You've got all that money. People have it all wrong about money don't they? all those telly millionaires looking craggy and sad and telling you how unhappy they've been. What a con. Well, I may have to work for a living but at least you can help me, said Katie. She balanced her guidebook on her knees, as she drank another coffee: Listen to this. They've completely rebuilt it. Warsaw I mean. As it was in the *1800s*. Can you remember at all how it was before the war?

To Lalka's surprise, her mind opened at the question. Was filled and over-flowing. With perfumed women, and soldierly men; she was walking across streets of droskies and push-carts, a child, holding someone's soft hand. She was sitting in yellow light at a marble-topped table. She could taste and smell. Honeycake. Cherry. Aniseed.
—What did you say? repeated Katie impatiently.
—I. Don't know, said Lalka slowly. She was so surprised: I mean, I think I realized we wouldn't be going back into the ruins. It's thirty years.
—You look a bit queasy, said Katie: Have a Kwell.
—No. That's not it.
Lalka looked round the room of decorously dressed travellers. It was spring, and they looked fit and expectant; their flesh was full and rounded. Lalka shut her eyes. Against her will now her mind was flowing like a river. Under the skin of every rounded body she could see blue cords and pouches. Veins, guts and blood. She shook her head to rid herself of the vision. Flesh waiting to fall into the grave. For a moment it seemed to her with horrible clarity that everybody seated at their separate tables might as well have been dead already.
—This is no way to start on a holiday, she said inconsequently.
—We shouldn't have had those cutlets, said Katie,

Never mind. If it's all blank, that's how it is.

And went on turning pages.

—I suppose the villages will be different, at least, she suggested.

The boat rocked.

—Yes, the villages. Wouldn't you think?

The villages. Narrow streets, wooden houses. And. Odours of mouldy potatoes, onions, kerosene. They were hiding. My mother's eyes were blue and watery, Lalka remembered. In an outhouse. There she was standing by a sink of deserted pots and, chipped plates. Where? Cold spider-webs. There was water in a butt, green with lichen. It was night. She could hear sick horses; smell their coats, that were pungent and sweaty with fever.

—I'm sorry. What did you say?

—I was asking about Pilsudski, if that's how you say him, said Katie, a little irritably.

—Yes. Well. Not so bad really as the Colonels who came after.

But who was the figure then who found them in their outhouse? Black, lean, with wild frightened eyes? Moving them on. She could smell a baby's wet knickers. She must have been carrying Clara, she thought.

She said nothing. Katie went on reading in silence.

Lalka remembered; of course, her father was already out of the country.

The boat docked. The train was waiting. But the cars

had to be unloaded, and the light had gone before they were off their boat and had found their carriage.

Katie sniffed as they entered the red leatherette compartment: Ash and coffee grounds, she suggested.
—With a few old orange skins, said Lalka. Other faces put their head round the door. She could hear pushing and jostling in the corridor outside. And the Tak-Tak-Tak of Polish voices.

Katie took off her jacket, and on second thoughts removed her brooch and put it in her handbag: How the hell do you turn these things into beds? she wondered.
—*Prozhin panie?* A burly grey-haired Pole, very red in the face, put his head round the door apologetically.
—My God are we sharing with men?
—I suppose so.
—What's he say?
—He's got a bad heart, said Lalka: He'd like an early night.
—What? It's not seven o'clock.
—He'll show us how the couchettes go.
—Oh. All right.
—That's his wife in the corridor, they're arguing with the conductor.
—But what about something to eat? They told me in London each carriage had a guard with cooking facilities.
—Lemon tea, I should think.
—I'll die.
Lalka said nothing. The smells and Polish voices had set her mind afloat again. She was in another train. Filled with racks of cases, baskets and sacks. People trying to sleep against headrests; a smell both sour and sweet of people's bodies. She was filled with yellow light. Outside was not Holland, safe, gentle Holland, but a long river. The Vistula. And the lights were factory lights, lying like

candles in the water. The train was moving and shaking. she could hear children crying. And brutal voices.
—*Zhydy. Zhydy.*
She woke herself, by force, out of the memory. Her mother's eyes. The hopefulness shining out from their gentle blue.
—Eat, eat.
Katie said : All right, I admit defeat. Let him in. I can't even see where the ladder fits.

At last they were arranged in their couchettes. The train was moving. Lalka lay on her back and stared up at the bunk above her. Fighting off sleep.
Katie tossed restlessly : Christ, I'll never get through the night. On this.
—You've been asleep.
—Have I? Are the Poles in?
—Yes, said Lalka : rolled up on top. Or he is.
—These blankets are so scratchy. You don't suppose they're full of ticks, do you? How can you sleep?
—I'm not.
And then they were at the German border.
—Passport Control.
Lalka felt nothing. She produced her documents.
—I wish we'd had a chance to see East Berlin, said Katie crossly : It's bloody raining, or we might see something through the windows.
She scrubbed at one to remove the condensation.
—You aren't there yet, said Lalka patiently.
—Of course.

—Passport Control.
This time Lalka must have been asleep, because when

she woke her heart was banging at the voice. The tone was different, she could hear that. Suspicious. What was it?

But it seemed to be only Katie's documents that interested him.

—Excuse me.

—What the hell?

The man shut the door bowing courteously. It occurred to Lalka parenthetically that the man had failed to notice the Pole curled up on his top bunk. She said nothing.

—Journalist? The German officer came back, waving Katie's passport querulously: What paper? Please.

—Oh, is that what's biting you. Relax. I'm woman's page, said Katie quickly.

It seemed to satisfy him.

—Look, said Lalka suddenly as the train began to move. Ill-lit, sombre, and beautiful, that part of Berlin beyond the wall that is visible from the railway, rolled past them like a film clip.

Katie whistled.

Then she said: Can you possibly do the same thing again for me when we get to Poland? If the journalist bit comes up?

—Have you no shame? teased Lalka: After all you said last month?

—None, said Katie: I like a quiet life.

They both woke again in Posnan.

9

They had been given a small flat on the outskirts of Warsaw. While Katie went to use the phone box near the lift, Lalka sat looking out at scrub, small shacks, allotments, pylons. Everywhere was flat as a board. Once there had been nothing here except for a few Florentine trees; now there were heaps of sand and narrow concrete cylinders. Down below, a few women and small boys were banging carpets on a line.

—Haven't you made coffee yet? Katie said, from the door: That phone has finished me. You put in a *zloty*, pull a lever and nothing happens.

—I'm sorry. The kettle boiled. I'll do it now.

—Just as well, it would have been cold. And it's foul enough anyway. My God, did you *see* what western coffee costs? We should have brought in giant tins of instant.

—What are you doing today?

—*We're* going out to lunch.

—*We*?

—To the Actors Club. Katie munched: One thing, I will say. The bread's good here. If nothing else. What did *you* get up to yesterday?

—Not much. Toured. You?

——Well. It was rather a bore, really. Some gap-toothed translator lady with black spectacles hustled me round the Old Town. As they call it. All a con, isn't it?

—Yes.

Mind you, even before the war, Lalka thought, the old town had been a sort of fairy-tale for tourists. Postilions in snuff-coloured livery. And the pigeons and the priests. As if all of them had been left over from a film set. But now the streets with old ladies sitting on low stools in the sun were no longer there behind the show; nor the twisting sidelanes. Svietojevska, Freka, Rybaki. Nor the eccentric old men, the cripples. Now all the walls were repainted; all the doors oak; façades gilded; frescoes restored.

—Poor cow, she walked her legs off for me. So about tea-time, when they have lunch here I took her to the Palace of Culture. You know, that great monster sitting in the centre of everything? Russia gave one of the bloody things to everyone after the war; hundreds of huge conference rooms and swimming baths. There's a restaurant. Funny place, with four ancient men playing tangos. All brown and purple marble. With a dancing bear on the frieze. We bored the knickers off each other.

—Who do you really want to meet?

—Oh, theatre people, actors, film men, you know. Nothing political, will you remember that at lunch, Lalka?

Lalka said: But they'll all talk politics.

—Well, but we mustn't start it. Anyway I don't believe you. We're meeting that man who made the marvellous nineteenth-century village film, remember? *How* do you say that? Yes, well, it was rather embarrassing yesterday, I was introduced to someone I thought must *be* him. Well, it sounded similar. Anyway, he had a balding head, and bright blue eyes and he was very friendly. We even had a *Blutsbruderschaft* ceremony.

—What?

—No blood, in Poland, evidently; just a lot of vodka and kissing. But a lot of vodka. I think perhaps I fell asleep

116

for a while. Poor bloody Poles – took about fifty phone calls for them to find out where I was staying. But awkward, really.

—What was?

—Well, you mutt, I left this bloke saying *see you tomorrow*, but it's not him, is it? The translator lady explained on the phone.

Lalka said: I wonder, do you know what happened to the Yiddish theatre? I looked it up in your guidebook, and it gives an address.

—What date's the book?

—1970.

—Should be O.K.

—Well, there's nothing there. In fact, all there is between rebuilt number 9 and rebuilt number 11 is a stretch of grass.

—Lalka, I should leave that alone, if I were you. I don't know exactly what happened here in '68, but I do know the paper wouldn't send *me* over then. I think the régime ran a bit wild on Jews in high places and didn't want a New York eye about, still less —

—All right, I'll behave, said Lalka thickly.

The Actors Club had a kind of dusty splendour. Nineteenth-century cartoons on green baize walls; deep armchairs and button-back couches in worn brown leather in front of the bar. One fine chandelier, the crystals cloudy as salt. It was rather like an ill-preserved Vienna, a piece of some lost empire of courtesy.

Though the courtesy remained. Their host, Konstantin, an official of the Writers' Union, presided over a small group of people waiting for them at the bar. He was a large flushed man in his late fifties, and his eyes moved over both women with the frank appraisal of a womanizer. Lalka moved under his stare uncomfortably; she sensed something under his jollity which betokened power. Probably he was an important figure in the Party. Deep in another chair, a wizened figure raised his head to nod up at them. She recognized the name of a playwright famous from the last years of the nineteenth century. Astonishingly, he too retained a flirtatious manner, though his eyes had yellowed under the pupils, and were crossed with tiny veins; the lines about his eyes still winked and twinkled, though the gaze itself was dull. A young poet from East Germany was bending over him solicitously; Lalka felt the twinkling was mostly directed at him. Everyone spoke English.

The table was ready for them, and they filed in after Konstantin, who beckoned the film director to sit next to Katie. There was carp in jelly, *chłodnik*, pancakes with sour cream. Two glass carafes of vodka appeared on the table before the food was ordered.

With Konstantin on her right, and Gunter the poet's attention turned wholly towards the playwright, she filled her own glass with the colourless liquid and drank. Quickly. It was very strong. Burning.

—And you are also a writer, Mrs Mendez, said Konstantin politely. Under the affability she understood he was not interested in her answer.

—No. I'm nothing, really, she laughed.

—A beautiful woman has no need, he murmured.

The words surprised her. It was a long while since anyone had spoken them to her. But she did not like his mouth. It was too red and thin. And his eyes were too hot.

—You know, he said to her confidentially, taking a glass of vodka himself: I have a little trouble with my heart. I have to stay calm. Tadeusz also. I am his medical adviser.

Konstantin nodded towards the film director.

—How odd, the taxi-driver who brought us here said the same, said Lalka, amused : It must be endemic in Poland. Heart disease.

—It is your vodka.

—Cigarettes, suggested Gunter.

—Fatigue, said Konstantin.

Everyone round the table laughed.

—I'm not interested in politics, she could hear Katie saying : my editor only wants to hear about your marvellous theatre and cinema.

—Who is interested in politics?, Konstantin shrugged : It is all old hat with us. Look at our young people. What interests them? Only music and clothes, and how possibly to get a car. The East German poet said : And censorship?

Konstantin made a little French wobble with his hands : *On se débrouille.*

Lalka had another drink. The carp was good, but very bony. She found herself eating with exaggerated care. Perhaps she was already a little drunk?

—That's right, isn't it, Tadeusz?

The film director smiled, and made a mocking gesture of dismissal with his hands. He leant over towards Lalka : You know, you shouldn't believe everything he says, he warned her : We are all a little afraid of him.

At her right, through the vodka, she could hear the hoarse, old voice of the playwright : So. They liberated Praga. On the left bank of the Vistula first. By September. Over here we watched. And they waited. House by house Warsaw burning down. And they waited. September to January. No, young man, I see things differently from you.

She did not catch the poet's next question, but it made the old man laugh until he coughed. He coughed; and then he lit another cigarette. As though his source of oxygen depended on it.

—Everyone has been in prison, he said eventually : And the man who put me in gaol. Because I was not enough Communist ? He is himself in America now.

Lalka took hold on herself. Ate more bread. How shameful it would be to collapse on her first outing. The jelly around the carp already tasted nauseous to her. When the meat came it was finely chopped; from the other end of the table, she heard a muted squeak of horror from Katie at the Polish version of fillet steak. For her own part, she was more disturbed by the difficulty she had in focussing. Eyes and ears. Already voices were beginning to weave about her hazily.

—The Czechs ? Yes, we are sorry for them, of course. But if they don't fight, if they aren't prepared to die . . .

—Do you think in 1970 the Russians didn't think of sending in tanks here ?

Lalka felt Konstantin's hand on her knee. But she did nothing. In a moment, when she could walk confidently, she would leave and find a lavatory. For the moment she allowed the stealthy fingers their way. Later. She could sort it out later.

—We Poles are all mad, the old man was saying to the poet, even as Konstantin edged up Lalka's skirt : it's our national asset.

Everyone agreed heartily.

And then Konstantin began to speak to the table at large and Lalka found herself suddenly alert. Tadeusz had mentioned the work of an old Jewish writer he wanted to film, and Konstantin was telling a story about one of his friends.

—During the war, he said he joined the German army. Yes. After everything is over in East Berlin, a middle-aged man recognized him. Don't I know you from

Warsaw? said the German. *Ja, natürlich*, said my friend. We met in the Officers' Club. But you, a Jew, in German uniform? And how else, my friend replied, but for the uniform, would I still be here?

Lalka could not laugh with the others. Her eyes met those of Tadeusz across the table. It seemed to her a flash of shared knowledge ran between them.

But now Konstantin was in full flight. It did not seem to bother him that Lalka had removed his hand from her knee.

—You know, once we had a lot of trouble, he was saying : Nothing must be, not even a little *little* bit, anti-semitic in our Theatre. So I remember. We wanted to put on a British play. And you know there is this figure – Goldberg, isn't it? The censorship wanted us to change his name. And take out this line and that. We argued.

—With himself, said Tadeusz from the other end of the table.

—Argued. At last, we won our way. We said. Look, the writer is a Jew. The man who wants to put the play on is a Jew. And you tell us what is anti-semitic?

Tadeusz said : Ah yes. I remember those days Konstantin.

—Ach, you with your Swiss money. What are you worried which days?

Lalka said, suddenly emboldened by the slight jar between the two men : I went to look for the Yiddish Theatre yesterday. It's gone.

—Oh, moved. That is all, said Konstantin quickly : They moved. And we subsidize them more than any other theatre, you know.

—They have to. Because there is no longer much of an audience now, said Tadeusz, looking Lalka full in the eyes.

—We even have to arrange simultaneous translation, said Konstantin irritably : But of course, it is a marvellous tradition.

—Kaminska is in Israel, said the German poet.

They had all placed her now. She could feel it. She could feel Katie's eyes upon her with reproach. Very carefully, then, she rose from her seat, and they watched her anxiously.

—What I would like, she said, her articulation strained to precision : is to find your ladies' room.

Green paint. Brass lock. Door shut. No-one else mercifully, in the grubby room. Her throat gurgled. Lalka was very sick in the basin. It had been foolish to drink so much so quickly. But at least, she reflected, feeling the muzziness leave her limbs, and concentrate itself in a pain at the base of her skull; at least I'll be sensible now. She washed her face several times in cold water. Her eyes still hurt a little when she moved them. She combed her hair. Pursed her lips. She'd looked worse, she thought, colouring her lips. She returned with a certain precarious aplomb.

—Here, Katie beckoned her.

Lalka sat between her and Tadeusz.

He spoke gently to her.

—Listen, he said : It is also hard to be a Pole. My mother died in a women's concentration camp. So I try not to think of it. My brothers were hung in Warsaw. But we drink a little vodka you know, and laugh. Even so.

—What else should we do? demanded the playwright : You have seen the camps? Six million Poles died in those camps also. Did you know?

Lalka said : I haven't seen the camps. Except. The photographs. Every one knows the photographs. But perhaps. She stopped : My family had a house in Krakow. I have the address. I plan to make a kind of. Trip of homage. That is all.

—When are you travelling, have you a car? said Tadeusz : I will take you there. I have to go down south anyway. Perhaps we can fly?

—I think I would like to drive, said Lalka.

She turned to Katie helplessly.

—But I don't want to interfere with your plans.

Katie's left eye lowered almost imperceptibly, and Lalka realized that, without meaning to, she had served a useful purpose.

—Sentiment before business, dear, said Katie, in a mock-cockney accent.

—Then we drive south tomorrow.

—You really intended to go? Or is it just to please us? Lalka asked uncertainly.

—I want to go, he said firmly.

There was more vodka for everyone. Lalka accepted the drink in her glass, but left it untouched.

—Five hours to Krakow? He must be mad; here, look at this map. There aren't even any mountains in the way.

—Perhaps he's thinking of traffic.

—What? There *are* no cars in this country. You can park in the middle of Warsaw, how are you going to fill a hundred miles of motorway?

—I doubt if it's motorway exactly.

—But it's flat. All Poland is flat.

—There he is.

The two women looked down from the window on Tadeusz' short figure, getting out of his car, looking even more like a teddy-bear in a belted camel coat. They were both packed and ready, but Katie was grumpy with headache, and enforced early rising. Lalka had woken spontaneously at first light; been washed and dressed before Katie staggered up; was humming over lemon-tea while Katie crashed round the bedroom looking for her long skirt. And Lalka knew why she felt so surprisingly awake of course. But she kept the knowledge bated. She kept herself still, saying I am too old for much, in any case, and I may be wholly mistaken. I mustn't be a fool.

—Jesus Christ, Katie said, getting into the back seat of the car decisively: whoever spread the lousy myth that vodka doesn't give you a hangover? How do you Poles *survive*?

—About three o'clock this afternoon you can ask the question again, said Tadeusz: The peasants will come off the land then. They begin work very early, you know. And when they finish they really do drink. In Warsaw, we don't drink hard.

—What else is there to see on the way? said Katie.

—We've left it a bit late.

—Late.

—To divert. You should really have seen Biskupin. There's a marvellous wood village in the bog there. Charred, three thousand years old. Marvellous. And Torun, the Vistula is beautiful in Torun. But we must try not to drive too much in the dark. So on the way, he smiled over his shoulder at her, you will see mainly forest. If you like, we can have lunch in the forest.

—With the toads and mosquitoes, said Katie ungraciously: I suppose.

—It's a lovely day, said Lalka: Let's do that. Shall we?

They drove out through suburbs of matchbox-shaped new apartment buildings, stucco-finished in brown, cream and green. The thin road stretched out before them. Tadeusz drove carefully. After only a few moments on the open road, he had to pull out sharply to pass a horse-drawn cart loaded with grass. The horse looked round slowly at them as they drew out.

—There's no one driving it, exclaimed Katie.

—Oh yes. Look. In the back. In the grass.

—He's asleep.

—That's all right. The horse knows his way.

—My God, What happens if you meet two of those things on the road at the same time?

—You slow up, said Tadeusz gravely, it happens quite often. Go to sleep. I'll tell you when it's time for lunch.

—Sleep? On a road where the horses do the driving?

Tadeusz laughed : The peasants need to sleep. They are tired. They work themselves to death. To send their children to university. To escape.

—That's interesting, said Katie : Can they?

—We have a points system. If you live in outlying areas, if you have illiterate parents and so on. Yes. It is possible.

—How enlightened.

—The system has made some problems. It gets quite hard for a teacher living in Krakow, say, to get his child into a good university. It makes for – how do you say in English *Protecsia*? he asked Lalka.

—We have the class system instead, she told him.

Trees. Silver trees. More carts. Katie lay back. The upholstery in the back seat was in German leather. Very comfortable.

—Your friend has gone to sleep, said Tadeusz, looking in his mirror : Do you want to? I shan't think it's rude.

—But I don't. Absolutely not, she exclaimed.

—Do you like our Poland?

—It's beautiful, she said : I'm afraid of how much I like it. Afraid it's sentimental. After everything that has happened. I still feel as if I had come home. And, she hesitated: I like you too.

He smiled at her. A friendly non-committal smile. She drew inward a little. And then he slowed to a stop for a group of peasants who were walking five abreast, as an entire family, across the road.

—Don't they get killed doing that?

—I don't suppose so. Can't be a large statistical risk.

—Your English is very good.

—Yes? I think better in French. Or German.

A little moody silence fell between them.

Then he said: You know I was married. Last year. To an actress in the *Stary Teatr*. She looked like you.

—Oh, I see. Lalka's breath caught.

—No. She was killed in a plane. Just like that. About six months ago. It happens, of course. But.

—I understand.

—Not yet. You see, I love Poland. I could live anywhere in the world, if I chose to. But I want to live *here*. I don't want to go to Hollywood, or Paris, or make films for the West like my friends. But my wife, she wanted to go abroad. She had never been. It's quite often the case here if a man goes abroad, they keep hands on his wife. So. When she heard she had her exit visa, she flew back to Warsaw in a friend's plane. For quickness. And then.

—That's terrible.

After a moment's pause, he said: Are you an actress in England?

—No, I never thought to be, said Lalka: but I had an aunt. She worked here. Before the war.

He cried out: Yes. I *know* her. She was in an early film. Yes. You have her good bones.

—I think it must take more than bones.

—Your soul is good for acting also, he said confidently: I

126

mean that. You change. From day to day, you are someone else. That is an actress' soul.

—I'd never thought of it like that.

—It's not too late.

—Absolutely it is, she laughed.

But what he said made her happy. How odd. Could
what she had always thought as a wobble of inconsistency
be a virtue?

—You're not putting me on? She checked herself.

He was puzzled. He didn't know the expression.

She explained, but it didn't matter. He wanted to
please; he had understood something real in her; she
was not deluding herself. Already there was something
between them. For a moment she wondered about
Katie in the back of the car. Quixotic bitch, she thought,
however could she be still asleep?

After lunch, and still a hundred kilometres from Krakow,
the light began to go.

—We ate too well, said Lalka apologetically.

—Wild boar, said Katie appreciatively: Fantastic. I wish
I thought I'd ever recognize it again or a menu. Do they
still run wild in these trees?

—Perhaps. Further east, said Tadeusz.

—My God, what's that?

An enormous frog hopped solemnly across the road.

—Do you even give frogs right of way? demanded
Katie.

—They have to live too. But look. There are other
hazards.

The families of people across the road were now more
numerous; and there were also crowds of men, evidently
drunk to the point of collapse, leaning on one another;
falling down occasionally; evidently oblivious of danger.

—Why do they walk like that on the main road to Krakow?

—Where else can they walk?

—They'd be safer in the ditch.

—They'd never crawl out, laughed Tadeusz.

As the car stopped a group of men surrounded it, dancing, laughing and pushing one another. Lalka felt a touch of fear. They were not peasants as she thought of them. Or had been taught to think of them. Their faces were narrow, not like Polish faces at all. Thin and lined meanly. When their mouths opened, their stumps of teeth showed black and ugly. Something in their manner was hostile rather than playful. And they brought back other memories.

—Don't be afraid, said Tadeusz quietly : They are only drunk.

One of them fell in the road, and two of his companions hoisted him upright. His head lolled forward, like the head of a crucified man.

—Oh God, said Katie : can't we get on?

—In a moment.

He hooted. The group parted for him at once. But now it was completely dark. He put up his headlights, which immediately picked out a horse and cart; unlit, and in their way; a hundred yards ahead. A squirrel ran across the path of the beam of light.

—From now it will be a slow drive, Tadeusz said : but don't worry. We have rooms. I already rang ahead.

Lalka must have been asleep, because the next thing she saw was light; yellow stone, and a square of floodlit arches. She knew it at once.

Katie said : We're here. And isn't it worth it? Did you ever *see* such a beautiful square?

—The Rynek, said Tadeusz.

—I know.

—I'll try and park.

As he drew into the kerb, a man in uniform knocked impatiently on his window.

—Now what's this, said Katie: Parking tickets? That's the Military, if ever I saw it.

But Tadeusz put his head out of the window and the two men exchanged words in a friendly tone.

—Nothing, he explained, winding up the window again: he was just telling me. Where my friends are eating, if we want to join them. Are you too tired after the trip? We'll find the rooms first, anyway.

—I'd like a wash, said Lalka uncertainly: but I'm not really tired somehow.

—Is that the hotel? I want to pee, said Katie: Can you see to my bag? If I just nip in first.

—O.K., of course.

She opened the door and was out on the pavement. A few passers by turned to stare at her. But Lalka felt her own heart begin to beat more quickly.

Tadeusz put his hand on her neck; a soft, gentle hand. She nearly cried out with the familiarity of it.

—How many rooms? he asked quietly.

She looked into his eyes. Brown. Serious. There was no ambiguity.

—Two, she said: if that's what you want.

She was immediately nervous. Perhaps she had spoken too quickly? But they were middle-aged, what was the point of coquetry? There was no time to question and dither. There would be no long term. They both knew that.

—Good, he said.

He bent across and kissed her softly on the lips. A full soft kiss, not sexy; a friendly kiss.

129

—We can see the others tomorrow.

She knew what Tadeusz would look like without clothes.
And so watched him undress, matter-of-factly, as if they
had known one another through a long relationship. He
was shorter than Mendez, but he had the same stocky, firm
body; no waist, no hips, no hair on his back; just soft
golden hairs on a broad chest; a line of gold running
down to his penis. She took off her clothes with the same
absence of either hesitancy or eroticism. It occurred to
her, for a fleeting moment, that both of them might lie
down calmly under the white soft quilt, like a married
couple, and just hold one another gently. Without any
sexual encounter.

And for a moment that was how it was. He held her
to him quietly. They talked a little. He lay on his back,
with an arm thrown behind his head. He said : Do you
trust your friend?

—Katie? I never thought of it.

—Writers, he said : they use everything. *Voyeurs.* Everything is useful to them.

—And what about makers of films?

—Yes, yes. We also follow people. Spy on strangers. Steal
conversation and gestures. Nothing is ever altogether
clean for us either. If something hurts us very much, we
say no, never, we will never touch or use that. Too close,
too much pain. But then it fills all our thoughts and our
dreams and at last we give in. We exorcize it, or pretend
to. But really we *use* it. And afterwards we live off our
treachery. He smiled : Remorsefully of course.

—Off your energy, said Lalka firmly : Some of us don't
have it spare.

Tadeusz sighed, and threw back the coverlet.

Lalka was glad to have him look at her; glad that her

breasts were large and white, and that her nipples pointed up sharply even as she lay on her back.

—You are very beautiful, he said.

He put his hand gently on one full breast. Kissed her.

—And very innocent.

—Hardly.

—You don't know about celebrity. Or don't care. It's very fine. Why do you want to sleep with me? I am not such a beautiful man.

—I feel at home with you, she said steadily: You seem familiar. I'm not afraid of you.

He stroked her gently.

—I am not violent, that is true.

Now she could feel his erection; knew he had been waiting for that; put her hand to him. For she was ready also. As she had never thought to be again.

They made love very simply; and fell asleep still wound in one another's arms.

—Where shall we go? The *Wavel*? The Church of which Mary? What do you think? Katie put the guidebook under Tadeusz' nose.

—What do *you* want to see? he asked Lalka.

Uneasily, she watched Katie making notes, as she read. And recalled again the dropped eyelid, the connivance of the other evening. Later she would have to ask Katie point-blank. What are you up to? What are you writing up?

—Let's wander together, said Tadeusz: How much do you remember of Krakow?

She confessed: Less than I thought. There is one street, isn't there, that leads down into Kasimiersh? I want to walk that way this morning.

—What's there? said Katie quickly.

—Kasimiersh? Well, it was once a little town. It was built by the King Casimir, because he fell in love with a Jewish girl, and made her his mistress. So he built a haven for her people, explained Tadeusz.

—And it became the ghetto?

—Never exactly, said Lalka : None of my mother's family lived there. But the poor Jews, yes. Once.

—And now?

—Now, said Tadeusz : There are no more Jews in Kasimiersh, though you know there are several thousand in Krakow. No. It is the poorest of the Poles who live in the houses of the poor Jews. Who are gone.

—I think I'll visit the *Wavel*, said Katie : And we'll go to the theatre this evening. Shall we?

—Of course.

Broken roofs. Red bricks showing under the plaster. Wooden doors stripped of paint. As they walked Lalka felt a growing cramp, which she tried to disguise. But it ran along her back and her arms, and she had to stop and catch her breath.

—Are you all right? Tadeusz was concerned for her.

—I suppose so.

Above them, where they stood on the cobbled street, a fat woman on a broken balustrade, was leaning and looking down. She shouted something. Lalka couldn't catch the words. But gradually the pain along her back and arms eased. She was able to stare about at the ruined walls; the rusting windows with flower-pots along them; tar-covered oilcloth hanging over broken tiles to keep out the rain.

—It is sad here now, said Tadeusz, watching her face.

—What else should it be?

—There's still a synagogue here. If you're interested, he

asked diffidently: Otherwise, perhaps I can drive you to the salt-mines; they have figures carved in salt, even chandeliers. Or –

—A synagogue? The Germans left it?

—Well, it's still standing. The government painted out the vilest of the German words on the walls. And recovered the bronze candelabra. You know, they had been taken to Berlin. It's very old. And, he hesitated: There is also a cemetery. If we can get the key.

—Please, she said eagerly: Yes, I would like to see.

The Hebrew words were still on the walls. But the doors were locked. It was impossible to see over the wall. Impossible to believe anything lay over the wall. As they stood, wondering, a few scraggy children came up to look at them. Giggled a little. Tadeusz laughed: They think we are Americans. It is the Americans who come here. They want to beg biro pens from us.

—I haven't any. Have you?

And then a taxi screeched to a halt at their side. A man with a red beard and wrinkly eyes scanned them as the children had. Knowingly.

—Americans? he said: You want to see inside? I can arrange. I know where is the Shamus. You like me to take you there?

Tadeusz said: Is it far?

—What is far? For Americans. Get in.

And from the front of the car he began at once to tell them his whole life story. Like a character from *Candide*. Lalka listened to the rapid chronicle of violence.

—So then, cut off altogether, I fight with the Russians. Up through the Ukraine. The whole war. Still, I was lucky. They passed a law to let us fighters come back.

Oh yes, I was lucky. It is not good for a Jew in Russia now.

—And in Poland? Lalka asked politely, because the pain in her side had returned. Like a bad stitch. Making it hard to talk.

—It is not so bad, said the taxi-driver: The papers say bad things, but nobody does much. For the moment. And, he laughed, also I am sixty. My family died long ago. And in Israel, he touched his nose, you have to work hard. Be strong man.

—The taxi-drivers must be the last pieces of private enterprise in Poland, said Lalka. And then laughed nervously because she was afraid Tadeusz would add something anti-semitic. But he did not.

The Shamus of the synagogue was pale, stoop-shouldered, ill. He came along without enthusiasm; as if he had been called on many times. And he spoke no English. At first he used Yiddish, then, placing Tadeusz, he made him an interpreter. They went through the stone wall.

Behind lay a thirteenth-century building. A synagogue. Restored, and mysterious in disuse. He let them in, quietly. Began to mumble the official history. The dates. Pointed out the candelabra, all made by local craftsmen, lovingly; each animal different on every hanging. It was a simple small-scale structure. Unlike the churches, the huge ornate churches of Poland's vehement Catholicism, which had frightened Lalka. So that in them, she heard the clip-clop of her heels profanely on other people's holiness. Here she felt she could enter and marvel. As of right.

The Shamus opened the delicate ironwork of the ark and showed them that the scrolls were missing.

—But he says they are safely in a museum, added Tadeusz.

—And the cemetery?

Outside the stones lay in profusion. The Shamus pointed out the famous old stones from the fourteenth century. Sirkis. Shapir. Samuel, doctor to Casimir. Pointing at each went the sad grey man, limping and tired. About the stones where the great Rabbis lay. Lalka followed.

—Can you read the carved stone?

Lalka was ashamed. She could not.

But suddenly the bodies lying under the stones seemed enviable; these men who had lain down quietly under the soil, often in their seventies; blessed by families and friends. Quietly. Without more than the ordinary pain of relinquishing life and going into darkness. Enviable. Lalka walked across a flat stretch of grass, out of which a few bushes pushed. No more. And thought, yes, how peaceful. To lie under the grass. Under the arbitrary weeds. Some flowers. A single rose.

And then the Shamus stopped: Here, he gestured over the flat expanse. An unknown number of people. May be hundreds. We don't know. Were shot by the Germans. It was before they realized shooting was not fast enough, he explained. Here. He waved over the grass.

Lalka gave a wordless cry. Tadeusz took her arm.

Now the bushes growing out of the soil looked sinister to her. There was blood in the grass. The weeds, the grass, and the rose all grew from that blood. It was horrible.

—I think that is enough, said Tadeusz.

But the Shamus was determined to finish his task. He showed them the wall, in which the names of the thousands who had been murdered by the Nazis had been etched. It was all that remained of them now, that golden etching. Lalka stared.

On the way out, Lalka fiddled in her pocket for *zloty* to give their guide. Brought out a few notes.

But the taxi man said, contemptuously: So little? That's soda-water money.

Lalka doubled the amount queasily. The little stooped man took it without offence. Bowed a little.

—He wants to know if you'd like to light a candle, said Tadeusz.

Lalka remembered now; the white wax blobs on several of the stones.

—No. Explain. It is an American custom. I don't recognize it.

The taxi-driver shrugged. He was disapproving.

—We will go now and have a drink, said Tadeusz firmly: It's enough. And your house we can do later. After we have eaten. O.K.?

—I take you back to the Rynek? said the taxi-driver.

—Well. Nearby. I booked a table, Tadeusz explained glancing aside at Lalka: at the Wierszenek. It is a good restaurant.

—Do they chop the meat?

—Chop? He did not understand: It's a good restaurant, for Poland.

—I don't think I *can* eat. I'm sorry.

—Eat a little.

—Yes, of course. Lalka didn't want to seem ungracious: But don't let's go somewhere very grand. Shall we go where your friends eat?

—If you like that better, of course.

—Perhaps you can explain I want something absolutely plain.

Then the taxi turned into a narrow street, and Lalka saw, incredulously, a small corner of a single square brightly pained. Four or five small shops there looked as though they were still in use, with fresh signs hanging over their doors, in Polish, Russian and Yiddish. *Hatshop. Tailor. Goldberg.* Other names. The names from the wall of golden letters.

—What's this? she cried: Stop. I don't understand.

Tadeusz seemed uncomfortable for a moment: A friend of mine. He is making a picture, a film you know? Of a book by Shulz.

—So they restore the past?

—We are good at it, they tell me. But look, in this case it is all film cardboard and pretence. There's nothing behind it. He laughed.

—No.

—He is a very great writer Shulz. Bruno Shulz. Do you know him in England? He died in 1939.

—I'm glad he should be remembered, said Lalka.

Yet the restored façades worried her, she could not have said why.

While they waited for their table, Tadeusz showed Lalka an enormous menu of food, and she shook her head at most of it.

—Fish, I'll have fish. Only.

—Look, I'll ask the waiter. About this *chopping*, said Tadeusz.

—No. I'll just have a glass of wine.

—The wine here is *not* good laughed Tadeusz: much better you have vodka.

—I can't, she said: I think I've poisoned myself, somehow. All right. One glass.

—Now we can talk. Tell me. When did you leave Poland? How?

Lalka said: In '39. Early. My father was already in

Rumania. He was preparing for us. You know, there seemed a time when it would be possible to live there? He had relatives. Everyone knew we had to go. Even in our own street there were many people ready to welcome the Germans. Because they hated the Jews.

Tadeusz frowned.

—But it was too late. In 1939 we had to run south with everyone else. Just the same. My mother had a ring she pawned. In Rumania we were helped by the Polish Refugee Board.

—And the relatives?

—They had already. Disappeared. Then the Iron Guard, she stopped : Why am I telling you all this. My husband. So often, she hesitated.

—I know. About your husband. His brothers were partisans, they have a small plaque even. You didn't see it in Warsaw?

—*How* do you know *who* my husband is? She said : What do you mean? Know?

—Everyone knows you are the wife of Alex Mendez.

—But I don't want that. She was indignant : When it is no longer even true. I have come here to be *myself*.

Indignation rose like black bile in her stomach; she had to contract the muscles of her oesophagus against it. And again there was a shaft of pain across her shoulder blades.

—Lalka, don't be angry.

—Well, it's very diappointing.

—Your table is ready, said the waiter.

They followed; a little distance between them.

—Ah, Tadeusz, I see you have found your leading lady, said a voice of great smoothness.

Lalka said : Oh no. I'm no actress. She was not displeased.

—But she is perfect. She *is* the part. No?

—Maybe, said Tadeusz.

Lalka stared at him.

—My God, you swine, she said: you're *studying* me. All the time.

—I warned you, I study everyone, he said gravely. Go away, Leszek, you meddler. All he means is you are beautiful.

—Yes. But perhaps as Jewess is beautiful? Yes. Someone escaped. Is that your film? Listen then, she said fiercely: Get this right. Since you know so much about me. My father spent his last years in a slum in London; my mother worked herself to death to feed us on too little money. Perhaps I was lucky. But my sister has worked her life away. Get that right. If you're looking for information. Don't. Don't cast us in mink, Tadeusz. We aren't all plump. Pick another face, another type. Haven't enough people died with mine? Or for mine?

—They died together. Rich and poor. Famous and ignorant. Look. Do I make Marxist tracts? Am I a fool? Haven't I been in the West? I told you, he said patiently: You are like my wife. She should have played the part, and she is dead. Lalka, if people want to hate, they will hate the poor Jews because they are dirty; and the beautiful because they are rich.

Lalka wanted to stand up. To get away. To go and wash. Instead, out of habit, she drank from the glass in her hand. And then the room flickered. The lights. The lights. She tried to make out the decorated wallpaper across the restaurant. It shifted; doubled. Her head sank forward. On to the cutlery. She felt. A fork in her forehead. A glass fell to the floor.

Around her she heard a babble of concerned voices.

139

10

—So there you are. An idyll. A displaced Vermeer. Tobias' voice mocked. He was leaning against the doorway to the music room, high up on the south staircase. The long window opened on to dazzling whiteness. Below there was nothing but sky, china-blue as a plate, holding in the heat of the invisible sun. The air hardly moved over the rockfall; and the leaves of the blue creeper at the window were preternaturally still. Framed in the golden section of that window, Mendez and Lee sat together at the harpsichord, while Mendez' blunt fingers picked out a piece from the Fitzwilliam sonatas. Lee hummed softly. Unselfconsciously. But she looked tired. She was dressed in white, with a gold band caught under her breasts, and a long skirt loosely flowing down over her distended belly.

When she looked up, two fine lines appeared at once at the sight of Tobias' aquiline face, and angular figure, poised on the threshold: Where's your embroidery? he asked her.

She flushed.

—And why are you so curmudgeonly this morning? Mendez did not stop playing, though he turned slightly to observe his friend: How pale you are. It's unhealthy. You should learn to relax a little in the sun.

—My skin peels too unattractively, said Tobias lightly. Mendez turned sharply: So. Now you are awake tell me. How are things in England?

—Don't you read *The Times* any more?

—Bombs in central London. Flying glass. Strikes. Is that friendly gossip?

—You mean news of Lalka? Doesn't she write?

—I haven't heard for a while.

Lee stirred restlessly: I *must* have a drink, Alex. Something cold.

—Tea is better.

—Lalka left for Poland a few weeks ago. Clara thrives, said Tobias.

—How?

—In a dress shop. But Peretz is ill again of course. Anything else?

—No, said Mendez moodily: Lee, shouldn't you take a rest now? Be a good girl.

She flushed: I'm not tired.

—Go, anyway.

—Tell me, said Tobias quickly, before she could stand up: Who are the gentlemen on the other side of the building? Sitting outside, drinking Pernod, and singing? Under my window.

—I hope they didn't disturb you.

—They're friends of mine, said Lee: Alex lets them crash here for a week or so.

—Lucky them. A very good pad, said Tobias: I wonder how you ever get them to leave?

—They go away, I've learnt, said Alex.

—Some of them, Lee hesitated.

—One or two, said Alex: are at least articulate. I'm sorry, Tobias. Does their noise account for your bad temper?

Lee rose, rubbing her back a little.

—It seems inappropriate. When everything else is so set up for the happy delivery, said Tobias: When is the baby due?

—June, said Alex steadily : It may be a little early.

Lee flinched.

—Are you having pain?

—No, she bit her lip. For a moment her tan looked like paint.

—Go on, go away. Sleep.

—How charmingly you take on the role of nurse, said Tobias.

—Oh, it suits me. I'm very happy with it.

Alex met Lee's eyes and smiled.

—I'm very happy altogether, he said : Surprising, isn't it? The world is full of surprises. Did you know they actually dug up some ancient dinosaurs eggs near here recently?

—I can't see why that should be exciting, said Tobias : Were you planning to breed them?

—I suppose, said Mendez : the truth is you have no faith in the mysteries of the earth at all.

—Nothing mysterious about dinosaurs.

—No. They passed conveniently away, and left the planet for men.

—Quite so, said Tobias.

—Must you say everything in that tone? cried Lee.

—Now tell me, said Mendez : what exactly you are doing here? Not that I grudge you a holiday. But never mind that. I'm more concerned to know. Why have you spent most of this year in London? Antwerp is where I based you.

—I have commuted to Antwerp. At my own expense.

—So I hear. You can evidently afford it.

—Alex, said Tobias neutrally : whatever your other source of news may be – paid, I imagine – you can't know me so little as to think I am cheating you?

—Not in any way I can detect.

—I see. But you no longer trust me.

—No. But I've always worked on instinct in such matters.

—Something of an unreliable guide, I'd have thought, Tobias said. His whiteness had become almost bloodless.

—It's served.

—And I wonder what your little girl-friend has put in your head?

—Lee? Mendez was puzzled: I don't discuss business with her. She has no feel for it.

—Then?

—You've been poking about, said Mendez crudely: Why? What are you looking for?

—Nothing for myself.

Alex laughed: Then why? You know very well, for example, that I sold out everything South African ten years ago. What are you researching? My biography? Or my defence.

—Perhaps defence is closest.

Mendez raised his eyebrows.

—Then what cleaning-up operation, exactly, is under way?

Tobias began to pace uneasily about the room. He seemed about to speak; checked himself.

—You are getting it wrong, he said at last: However, if that's how you feel. You can get rid of me easily enough.

—I didn't say that, said Alex impatiently.

Tobias pulled his long chin thoughtfully.

—All right. Let me ask you again. Who are all these hippy characters lying about downstairs? Do you know? Alex shook his head in bewilderment: Of course. There is an unemployed Australian actor; and two singers from the fête last week. Those two had talent. The black child belongs to one of them, but I forget which. The grizzled American writes pieces of music.

143

—Have you heard them?

—He is too neurotic to let me. But he's quite charming sometimes when he's sober. And his wife is asleep.

—Alex, why? What are you keeping them all here for?

—My dear Tobias, it's an excellent arrangement. It saves Lee driving back and forwards to Aix. They don't disturb me.

Tobias hesitated: And what is your instinctive reaction to Jack Lacey? Precisely.

Alex smiled: Oh, I know all about Mr Lacey.

—But, of course, he's harmless.

—Not exactly.

—Then you're just keeping an eye on him, are you? asked Tobias: It doesn't occur to you to do more than that?

—I should have thought you'd approve of Lacey. Almost your mirror-image, Tobias, wouldn't you say? But Mr Lacey isn't in the château at the moment. He is staying with friends. In the Camargue. He is a gentleman who likes to ride powerful white stallions, and this is hardly the countryside for it.

—And Lee admires his horsemanship?

—He upsets Lee, said Mendez quietly: that's why I sent him away for a while.

—And you mean he just went? cried Tobias: Just like that?

—Well, naturally. What else could he do?

A buzzer went in the wall.

Alex lifted the receiver: Yes. I am holding, he said.

A line of anxiety creased the flesh between his eyebrows.

—Krakow, he said to Tobias. There was a question in his voice. Tobias signalled back total ignorance.

There was a long silence.

—Hello? said Alex impatiently: Yes, naturally. Mendez

speaking. Who? Katie. Well, hello, Katie. Yes. I can't hear you very well.

Then he listened attentively,

—I see. Do you need money? Who is looking after her? Of course. I will take a plane at once. Of course at once. Thank you for telephoning.

He put down the receiver, and began to walk about the room.

—What's the trouble?

—Lalka. She's ill.

—Shall I make arrangements for you? You'll need a visa.

—No. I have a friend in Marseilles. It will be quicker for me. But Tobias. Alex hesitated. His voice sounded strange : Listen, give me your word. Look after Lee. Look after the child in her.

—You expect Lacey to return.

—If he does I don't want her bullied.

—Very well, said Tobias, rising : I'll make arrangements to stay. I don't know what kind of a bodyguard I shall make, though.

—Lalka is very ill, said Alex : I may be a week. Or more.

—I'm not sure, said Tobias : that Lee will accept my protection. She's always thought of me as the enemy. Hasn't she?

—Well, she's not stupid, said Alex : You might have to alter your tone a little, do you think you could manage that?

—She's like a little ferret, mused Tobias : I've never been very good with jumpy small animals. With teeth. But I'll try.

—That'll do. Go and find her now, said Alex : while I organize a visa. Go on. You may enjoy it. You found her attractive once, didn't you?

—However that may be, said Tobias wryly : she certainly never took to me.

The terrace was silent. Tobias shrugged. Evidently Lee's friends preferred the dark side of the château. In a way, he agreed with them; the gorge, falling downward between uncut stones was more dramatic than Mendez' fountain. As he followed the path round the great house towards the sound of voices and music the sun was suddenly cut out by the shadow of a white cliff. Then he could see a three-year-old child, crouching in the scrubby earth, by a dry stone wall; his hands cupped. He was very still; his thin buttocks tensed; a line of small bones visible in a curve down the naked back. Tobias guessed he was hoping to catch either a lizard or one of the large grass-hoppers, whose legs kept up an incessant buzz in the dry air.

None of the others in the hollow of scrub above the gorge paid the child any attention. Lee, slightly apart from the others, had brought out a pile of cushions and was evidently asleep on them. If she heard Tobias' footsteps, she gave no sign. But she may well have heard nothing. The music and the voices alike, Tobias now saw, emanated from a large red cassette in the grass. Nobody seemed to be talking to anybody.

With some diffidence, Tobias approached a couple sitting with their legs over the drop, staring separately into the hollow of bramble, brushwood, and a few bushes of red hawthorn. They were older than he had expected, and both of them naked to the waist. The woman, whose expression was almost entirely hidden by huge black sunglasses, patted the powdery earth at her side phlegmatically. The man had a thin, wolfish face and looked pale and jumpy. It occurred to Tobias that he had interrupted not so much a quarrel, as a long-drawn-out sulk.

Averting his eyes delicately from the woman's low-slung breasts on their rubbery sinews, Tobias sat down as he was bidden in the white dust. In the hollow below he could see the bright purple shirt of a younger man asleep in the sun. The woman too stared down without speaking, but the man at her side handed over a deep green bottle of wine and said: Welcome to Paradise! With the soft purring accent of a Californian.

Immediately the two black circles of glass shifted their attention: Listen to him, she said contemptuously: Some Paradise.

Her companion began to make an attempt to open a second bottle of wine.

—Shit, isn't there anything you can do without help? she said impatiently.

—Lu, I think this guy's part of the management.

—Yes, I work for Mendez, said Tobias quickly.

—Well, I call that very democratic. Letting the servants out here too. Wouldn't get that in Italy. Irwin and I had some very bad experiences in Italy. What that country needs, said Lu complacently: is a few bombs under a few fat arses.

—I believe it's had one or two in its time, said Tobias.

—No, but I mean a real Revolution, you know. That's a sick society.

—March on Rome and all that, you mean?

—Well, I read a book once, and it could be we have had this Mussolini all wrong.

—Yes, well, said Tobias: his views are rather well known, really .I don't want to seem rude, but are you friends of Miss Walsh?

—Who? Oh, I know who you mean. No. Can't say we really take to that little girl, do we Irwin? It was some guy picked us up on the road. Lacey his name was.

Brought us on. Seemed to think we could rest here a while while we got things together.

—What sort of things, inquired Tobias: Do you get together?

—Well, Irwin's a composer you know. Uses short-wave radio, and tape. Very *avant garde*. Gets his music out of the air.

—I remember, said Tobias, without enthusiasm. A friend at Oxford had tried to explain a similar concept some ten years back.

—But Europe's so behind, I don't suppose you'll be interested. Behind – it's the dark ages. And *sexist*. My God. Do you read the papers here? You know that guy who stuck a breadknife in his wife last week? Well, the defence dug up the fact she once called him a sexual failure, O.K? And the whole jury burst out crying for him. I mean he was *acquitted*, for chrissake. Wow, she shook her head from side to side: think of that. Some poor chick has a guy look her up and down and say darling as far as I'm concerned you are just unfuckable. Every guy in court would look her over and say, The man's right. Give her an extra twenty years.

At this point Irwin stood up. Not in indignation, but to give himself more of a hold on the corkscrew. For a slow moment Tobias realized how drunk he was, and how close he was to the edge. Then he was over. Rolling down the hollow to the sound of broken glass, and a muffled squawk of pain, then perching for one second on the dip over the gorge. With horror, Tobias realized that his body had gathered enough impetus to roll further. Irwin did. And was out of sight.

—My God, said Tobias, appalled: he'll be smashed on the rocks.

The man below, who had been roused by the unexpected figure, sat up bewilderedly. Tobias began to clamber down the powdery slope towards him; slipping a little himself, and hearing the tearing noise of his trousers as they caught on stumps and thorns. He and the sunbather reached the rim of what was almost a crater together and peered over fearfully. But Irwin had not fallen far. He was caught in the gnarled arms of a cypress; helpless, thin, absurd, but evidently uninjured, his arms flailing wildly.

—Don't move, called Tobias.

—You mad? Look down there. You asking me not to *move*?

—Don't look, advised Tobias : just lie back.

—Listen, I don't want therapy, I want a rope.

The sunbather took his jeans out of a pile of sand, and gave them a tentative pull.

—These look pretty firm, he said : Don't you think?

Tobias felt the sun on his neck.

—I've no idea, he admitted.

Irwin sneezed : For Godsake hurry up, he shouted.

Mutely they dangled the jeans in his direction. He was more agile than he looked. Within a few moments he was back on the comparative safety of the first slope. Then he looked behind him.

—Shit, he said with disgust : I lost a whole bottle.

Tobias went across to Lee lying on her cushions, and said : I suppose you've seen Alex by now. He'll be gone about a week, you know.

—Yes.

The cassette started up loudly again. The same track. Tobias sighed; and brushed, rather hopelessly at his torn trousers. She opened her eyes at the noise, and began to laugh.

—You look as if you'd fallen into a flour mill.

Encouraged, he squatted at her side. Listen, he said quietly : do you think Lacey will more or less go on riding about the Carmargue indefinitely?

149

—No, she said : Do you?

—Not if he hears Alex has gone, said Tobias : On the other hand, I can't see how he will hear. Can you?

She didn't answer.

—Extraordinary company we have, he said conversationally; nodding across at the others : Any chance of shifting *them*, would you think?

—Not easily.

—No, agreed Tobias : How would it be if I gave them a bit of a *push*? Might make things quieter for you.

She opened her eyes again, and smiled : How pleasant you're being. Wonder why? Well, thanks, it doesn't matter. I quite like having a few people about, as it happens.

She held up a hand to him.

—Expect I'll see you again. Afterwards.

—Well, yes. You will, said Tobias awkwardly : I'm staying behind, you see. To look after things.

At once she sat bolt upright.

—What things?

—Well, anything that might upset you.

—Nothing's upsetting me.

—That *might* upset you then.

—Like what?

—If you trusted me I'd explain.

—Don't trust anyone.

—Not even Alex?

—Well, I know he wouldn't *hurt* me, of course. But I'm not stupid. I don't expect things to go on and on. Why should they?

—Well, that's fascinating, said Tobias : Where would you put Lacey? On your scale of permanent loyalty, I mean.

—Well, he won't disappear on me, said Lee, a little gloomily : He's just waiting about, that's all.

—And supposing he rides up now in Lawrentian white jodhpurs, what then?
—Oh I'd tell him to fuck off, naturally, she said, surprised.

There was no call from Krakow that night; or the following day. The Americans said they were thinking of moving on, but did nothing about it. The purple-shirted man in the hawthorn bush turned out to be a famous Monteverdi singer, and left quite briskly for an engagement in Paris. After he had gone, no one seemed to be sure who was responsible for the child. Tobias found the only way to prevent the boy from hurling himself from either battlement or steep cliff face, was through more or less continuous supervision. It was very tiring. After a day of it, he delegated the job to one of the kitchen maids; who took it as a god-given excuse to sleep in the sun instead of peeling vegetables.

Lee grew more and more listless. The doctor, who saw her daily, was worried about her blood count; wanted to take a piece of bone-marrow from her breastbone to see why his iron injections were having no effect. Lee held out for almost an hour; and then capitulated miserably. Tobias felt his own breastbone, just over the heart, thin as shell; and understood her reluctance. But the results were evidently reassuring. Tobias took it upon himself to make her take Vitamin B 12 tablets after every meal. They often ate together: Lee, Tobias, the black child, and the sleepy kitchen maid. No one talked much.

It was not until the third day of Mendez' absence that Jack Lacey reappeared. At the front door, dressed casually, in the least melodramatic way imaginable. With such a spontaneous smile; such a clean-featured, good-looking, boy's face, Tobias felt rather foolish at his own secret and elaborate precautions.

—Good heavens, Ansel? Lacey's voice rose with incredulity: What are you doing here? Are you having a nervous collapse?

—Never have them, said Tobias, coldly: and I might ask you the same question. Since I thought you'd left for more exciting games.

—Come back to see my friends, of course. Working on a book at the moment. Thought Mendez could help.

—A book? asked Tobias: What book?

—On the diamond industry. Show you my contract if you like. Aren't you going to let me in?

Tobias hesitated. Really, it seemed impossible to do anything else.

—If you want an account of the Mendez holdings, he said stiffly: they aren't kept here, you know.

—Oh don't be so shrill, Tobias.

—What do you want? Exactly?

—Well, I'd really like a look at his library, said Lacey.

—It's locked.

—Oh come on, he never locks anything.

—I'm sorry, said Tobias, curtly: I locked it for him.

—Look it's all genuine research. I'll show you my contract, if you don't believe me.

Tobias said: All right then, show it me.

Lacey paused. Then giggled: Funny old Ansel, all right. But aren't you going to offer me a drink?

—I suppose so.

—Very gracious. Lacey laughed: Well, at least you aren't hopelessly flabby, like most of the idiots I meet with money.

—In my experience, said Tobias: there are very *few* idiots

who keep hold of real money. Its quite easy stuff to disperse, you know.
—And the soft and the squashy and the flatulent? said Lacey.
—Go under.
—Not this side of the Revolution they don't, said Lacey : And you know it. Now, where's that drink? You *do* drink I suppose?
—Moderately.
—How is Lee?
Tobias said : Sleeping.
—At this hour? Lacey's eyebrows and his voice rose together with incredulity.
—Doctor's orders.
—Well, when *does* she get up?
—It depends. Come in. What do you want to drink?
—Something vulgar and harsh. Say, whisky with ice in it.
—Fine. Tobias laughed. Relaxed. Because suddenly the boy's youth and good looks made him a welcome change from the rest of the guests. Whatever his intentions. He liked the edge on his voice; the precarious vehemence.
—You see. *We'll* get on quite well, said Lacey. Perceiving as much.

They moved to another, cool, stone-floored room; and sipped their drinks together silently. Apart from an almost schoolboyish inability to sit straight on a chair, Lacey seemed relaxed and good-humoured.
Tobias said : Look. I'll change the lunch arrangements. There's a lost child we'd otherwise be feeding spaghetti into.
—Fine. What shall we do till then?
　Tobias registered the energy, the fear of boredom, the

sense of time as commodity. Recognized it. Felt morally obliged to meet the challenge of it.

—Chess? he suggested, doubtfully.

—All right, Lacey said: Though I'm not very good. I say, do you think ther's anything I could eat more or less right away? Hunk of bread and cheese would do; there's not much scope for breakfast, driving through this desert.

—Of course, said Tobias. He felt rather ashamed. Almost unconsciously he found himself adopting the paternal, indulgent voice of an Oxford tutor, dealing with a bright, complex student; a boy who needed guidance. He buzzed for a servant, with some confidence. Then caught his own mood. And suddenly remembered Mendez. *Who had asked him to stay.* Mendez, who feared no one.

—What are you carrying in your briefcase? he said to Lacey abruptly: Your manuscript?

—Not mine.

—Not?

—But you might like to look at it all the same. I think it's rather a find. Probably valuable. Did you know, said Lacey: Mendez' *père* died in Provence?

—Yes. Very sensibly on the move I should think, said Tobias warily: until cancer caught him. I believe he had some plan to set up Alex as a farmer. Of course, the married sons were left behind in Poland.

He watched Lacey open the briefcase, which contained an old, brown-edged exercise book.

—What's that? he asked quickly: And whatever it is, let me tell you, Alex buys nothing. Never has.

—Not even his own work? It's a diary. Look. Alex aged fifteen. Written in Provence.

—In what language?

—I had it translated.

—Did you know? said Tobias: With what end in view?

—Insight, you know. Into the prodigy. That sort of

thing. He writes well. Anyway, here it is. The typescript stuck inside is the translation.

—You mean you aren't selling it? said Tobias, stupidly.

—Good heavens, Tobias. What a very low opinion you have of me.

Against his will Tobias flicked open the book. It was mainly in note form; personal notes; the odd chess problem. An occasional cryptic sentence suggested reading habits unusual in a young boy. *Diamond as daimon.* Tobias shut the book hastily. Met Lacey's amused eye.

—I have a low opinion of most people, said Tobias.

Nevertheless the next few days passed pleasantly. Lee kept to her room, and Tobias was glad of Lacey's company. As far as he could tell, Lacey made no attempt to reach her. Mendez phoned, from Krakow, twice in one day; and the calls appeared to revive her spirits as far as Tobias could judge. He avoided one or two newcomers to the group of sunbathers. From habit, he still padded about the château at night; not so much now from anxiety, but from a hopeless insomnia which the old house with its creaks and empty spaces had begun to generate in him. He knew Alex was planning to return after the weekend. He had not spoken much of Lalka. Tobias walked and thought of that; and of Mendez' diary, still unread. And of Lacey. As his mirror-image.

The next morning Lacey came out on to the terrace, looked across at Tobias as he sat drinking coffee in the shade, and burst out laughing.

—For goodness' sake, said Tobias disgustedly.

He had fitted himself out for comfort in long white shorts and an aertex shirt, and was perfectly aware of the resemblance this gave him to some member of a lost Imperial Clubhouse.

—Well, you must admit, said Lacey: it's all a bit Edwardian. Especially the panama.

—A hat is common sense. I dislike heat on the back of my neck.

—Are you feeling athletic?

—Certainly not.

—There's a river about five miles east of here. We could go for a swim.

—It's probably full of sewage.

—The locals use it.

—I should think they're immune to anything.

—Come on, you aren't in Bechuanaland.

—It so happens I've some work to do, said Tobias rather huffily.

Later, however, when Lacey appeared in neat black swimming trunks, carrying a towel, Tobias looked up, and said a little sheepishly: Is there any shade there, do you know? I blister very easily.

—Willowy as the Isis, assured Lacey: and running cold and fast to boot.

Willowy it was not; but the curve of the river made a natural, if pebbly beach area; and there were very few other swimmers. At this early hour, the water lay in the shade of a limestone outcrop, in which a few sharp grasses, and a few olive trees had managed to root themselves. The water itself was clear, and unexpectedly deep.

Tobias swam with a dignified frog-stroke, keeping his mouth out of the water, and moving in a series of slow meditative circles, while Lacey crossed and recrossed the stream against the current with a fast overarm crawl. There was no wind, and the water was surprisingly cold;

156

much colder than the sea at the coast. The sound of moving water in Tobias' ears was like a forgotten piece of childhood. He stayed in longer than he intended, and was shivering when he got out; quite glad to fling himself on a slab of ground already heated by the sun. But he wrapped a towel carefully over his body and neck, and lay face downwards. Lacey lay on his back, his lean body fully exposed in total relaxation.

Sleepily from this position, he said to Tobias: Do you suppose, if I sold a few *œuvres*, and let you play with the money, you could make me a million pounds?

—No, said Tobias.

—I didn't think so. How *do* people? How did Mendez?

—You'd better ask him, hadn't you?

—Well, he did once start to explain. About traditions of rose-cut stones, and underpaid genius craftsmen in seventeenth-century Antwerp, but he rambled off the main point, I thought. I don't feel he took my question very seriously.

—He probably felt Marx had got there first.

—Tobias. Don't you feel any social responsibility at all?

—Yes, said Tobias moodily: But I've had too much sun. Let's get back, shall we? I think the main responsibility I feel is towards preserving normality. As I see it, the main trouble with your generation is, you've never seen it break down.

—Nor has yours. How do you know you wouldn't like it?

—It wouldn't help anyone. Things would just get nastier.

—How about for the classes underfoot?

Tobias stood up: They wouldn't like it any better under anyone else's foot. I think we'd better get back now.

—Worried about Lee? teased Lacey: Quite fancied her once, didn't you? Of course, she was boyish then. Pity she had to breed, don't you think? Not her style at all.

I I

She had been buried already by mistake. Still alive. And
then uncovered; taken out of the ground, with the earth
still sticking to her skin. Her breathing body put between
white hospital sheets, while they washed the huge swollen
lump on her leg. There were worms; worms in the white
flesh. They died under the swabbing; or some of them
died. The rest lay waiting in the pus. The whole swelling
was a hive of their eggs.

As Alex began waking up, aware he was on a plane, but
still gripped in horror he puzzled who? Whose was the
old body taken so unceremoniously back from the grave?
He had hardly known his mother. When he thought of
his childhood it was his father and his brothers he
remembered. His brothers. Who had gone through war,
hunger, typhoid, death. Reuben in the woodshop, laughing; wearing a sleeveless sheepskin coat. A huge lout of a
man; good-natured, but with no time for bookishness.
His wife was thin and narrow-nosed, Alex remembered,
with angry eyes; she spoke Polish and Russian well.
Slothful about the house, she always had time to answer
Alex' questions. But Alex' own mother? He could
hardly remember her face.

Alex wondered what was left of the Warsaw suburb
where Reuben had his factory. His loft, rather; precari-
ously timbered; smelling of sawdust and the pungent

glues, boiled in enamel pots. The whine of the saw shook the whole building. And below? Upholsterers, dyers, and one or two goats. Fed on potato peelings by Reuben's wife.

All gone, of course and Itzhak too. Sallow-faced and old; unmarried; the only one without the Mendez good looks. Well, well. They were all gone. With the Hassids in their caftans, who wouldn't eat egg with so much as a bloodspot; and the rich in their cafés, gold teeth glinting. The scholars, the bibliophiles; and the ladies who wore their amber talismans and slept with the book of Raziel under their pillow. Gone.

—We are coming in to land now.

Alex fastened his belt, moodily. The clouds beneath him looked solid. Like snow. It was summer; but his mind was filled with icy trees and purple shadows.

As he was changing his Orbis vouchers he heard Katie's unmistakable voice. There she was. Black jumper and floral skirt. Taller than any woman in sight. She approached him, with both arms held out, and took his shoulders firmly; drew his face to her cheek.

—How *clever* of you to get here so fast, she said: The travel agency we went through took *ages* over everything.

—Not all clerks are bastards, said Alex: Next time use the Embassy. How is Lalka?

—Now Alex, her voice dropped: whatever happens, you *must* promise me not to bully her.

—Are you mad? inquired Alex coldly.

—Well, bully. That's a badly chosen word. I just mean ... push at her. You know. Try and find out things, if she seems evasive. I just want you to know she couldn't stand it.

Mendez became aware suddenly that there was a

small, yellow-haired man at Katie's side, shuffling the toe of one elegant shoe awkwardly.

—Tadeusz, I'm so sorry. This is Lalka's husband.

The two men greeted one another, and Tadeusz intervened hastily: I wanted to explain. You must forgive me. The hotels here are all full with some absurd Pan-Slav Congress. I really made fifty phone calls for you yesterday to try and find you anywhere comfortable. But I have a room myself, in a goodish hotel: will you take that? I can easily stay with an actor friend of mine.

—You're very kind, said Alex slowly.

—My car is outside, said Tadeusz: I can drive you now to the hospital. Then, if you will forgive me, I must go. Because I must fly to Warsaw. Television. But of course you can keep the car.

Alex hesitated: Thank you. Perhaps, as we go, one of you will answer my question? What *has* happened to Lalka?

—Oh it's still so uncertain, cried Katie: Don't you see? The first day we all thought she'd just had too much vodka. I mean she was white and sick and sweaty. When Tadeusz called me I thought what a hoot. How embarrassed she'll be in the morning. And she was, of course, and stupidly apologetic; but she went on being sick, so we began to think it must be food poisoning. Which wouldn't be farfetched – wait till you try the food. Anyway, we called the doctor. Well, *he* took one look, and had her out in the van for the hospital before anyone could say anything. That's when I called. It looked like a stroke, you see.

—And now?

—They don't seem to know.

—Ridiculous. Come on; there must be a very simple test to establish whether someone has had a stroke.

—Of course there is. But there are hundreds of other

things to test for, too. They've shaved her forehead, Alex. Promise you won't seem to notice that.

—My God, what sort of monster do you think I am?

—Not monster.

—What then, *fool*? Alex was irritated.

He slammed the door getting into the car. For a moment a wholly unreasonable, shameful, resentment of Lalka shook him. Damn it, had he treated her so badly? Maybe they had quarrelled; but had he ever been vicious towards her? What lies had she told Katie?

Katie sat with him on the back seat, and put her hand softly on his arm: People react very selfishly to illness. I do. It frightens me. I'm only trying to warn you.

—I'm sorry, Alex said sharply, not to be put off: You've shifted your ground completely saying that. It wasn't what you meant. But it isn't important. Tell me. Can she talk?

—Yes.

—Slurred voice?

—You can understand what she's saying. It's more her mind. It keeps wandering off. She's in a kind of delirium without having a temperature. Oh, Alex, I blame myself, really. She wasn't really up to it, and I was curious. You know, her family had one of those marvellous houses a few streets away from the Rynek. And it's still there. Well, Tadeusz got us in; you see, he makes films.

—I know who he is, said Alex moodily: I saw *Forests*. Lovely. The old woman crossing the swamp, and the birch trees. So? When you got in?

—Well, it's a lovely house. High ceilings and yellow wooden floors. Every room has a different family in it.

—Why not? Why should that upset her? Her own family got away, didn't they?

—I'm not explaining well. It began before. Tadeusz had a rehearsal, so someone from the *Literatov Polskich* took us round. And before he knew anything he pointed out the house and said : That one was a *Jew* house. A *Jew* house ! It was horrible.

—Oh for Godsake, said Alex : have some sense. That's just a failure of grammar. Stop rambling, can't you ? Then *what* ?

—Alex, I've been at the hospital all morning. Just sitting. And listening. And trying to understand. Maybe I haven't got it right, Alex, O.K. Say what you like to me. But don't talk to her like that. Will you.

Alex wound down the window and stared out.

—You never did understand her, you see. What she needed. How frightened she was. How she trusted you. And now she talks about you all the time. Only about you. I tell you, I'd never have risked bringing you here otherwise.

—You don't approve of me ? said Mendez ironically : But are there any men you do approve of ? Except in so far as they're useful to you.

—I see. You mean you've never forgiven me for that story. All those years back.

—No, Katie, I mean something more general. I've always known, you treat all men as objects. They're either useful or not.

—You're wrong, Katie said, passionately : wrong as you *could* be. I'm a hopeless romantic, that's my trouble. What you say is just a marvellous sick joke.

—So you believe. Or say.

—Look. I don't give a fuck what you think of *me*. But I do care how you treat Lalka.

—I've hardly come all this way to torment her.

—Did you ever *mean* to ?

—No. Of course not.

—But that's what you did, she cried : don't you even know that ?

Alex checked himself: All right, all right, he said uncomfortably: perhaps I know what you mean. Just don't stand between us, don't come in and put your eye on us. That's all I ask. There *is* a bond, he said heavily: bound to be. After all those years of life together. Don't insult me, Katie. I wouldn't hurt her now.

—I'm told you live in France, said Tadeusz from the front seat.
—For a homeless cosmopolitan, teased Alex: it's as good a choice as any.
Katie said: Alex. Don't you know in Poland they feel they have real ties with Paris? I don't mean just Chopin and all that. These people really feel they're the last outposts of European culture, keeping the Asian hordes at bay.
—Well, if you went further east, in St Petersburg, said Alex: You'd find the same thing. Perhaps it's even true. The barbarians are always further off. To the east.
—You couldn't live under Socialism though? asked Tadeusz.
—In Poland? Where it's corrupt? Why not? Until they winkled me out, Alex grinned: But you can be winkled out anywhere. At the moment I have the feeling of a certain lenience here. People don't look frightened. I suppose it changes. Year to year. I talked to a man on the plane who comes every year from America to visit his mother. He said he felt safer in Warsaw than New York.
—But he goes back, nevertheless.
—Habit.
—We have a lot of petty thieves, said Tadeusz: If you had a Western car they would steal your wing mirrors, if not your wheels. And some of the men who offer to change your money are informers. If you like, Tadeusz

said diffidently : I can change for you through PKO.

—Exactly. You will look after me, said Alex : You see? That is how I know I am in Central Europe. It is just not a Western convention to attend to strangers. Like Poles do.

—How about in Ireland? suggested Katie.

—Perhaps.

A rare hostility shook Alex. And yet he could see Katie too was looking haggard. Unlike herself. Her arms straight to her sides, her fists clenched. Her long eyes, without make-up, were no longer an intense green. Alex glanced from Katie to Tadeusz; calculating their relationship. He concluded it was not close.

—Is the hospital adequate? he asked.

—Yes.

Tadeusz fell into Polish : You are from Warsaw not Krakow, I know. But there is a good medicine here too. Alex hesitated : I am *glad* she's not in Warsaw. Too many of my family died there. All my brothers. I don't know exactly where they died. Or their families.

—Reuben Mendez was a partisan though. Isn't that right?

—Yes, said Alex gloomily : He was lucky. But then he was a notable man; rich, not one of the richest perhaps, but in his position he could have been part of the *Judenrat*. The mediators, the voices of quiet. Instead he organized the first smuggling into the ghetto. Food. Guns. He was one of the first to prove that Germans could be shot, could bleed and die in the streets like Jews and Poles. So when the ghetto fell, he was also one of the few to reach the forest. But it was not a matter of survival by then.

Tadeusz said : Perhaps my brother was one of the same group of partisans.

164

—Not so common, commented Alex : for Poles to fight with Jews.

—After the ghetto fell, some of us understood. We had seen the last fighters firing from their bunkers. In the forest we remembered.

—Yes, said Alex : my brother was lucky. He died in the trees.

Tadeusz said : Very lucky. They hung mine on a butcher's hook.

—You are a Catholic? asked Mendez.

—Yes.

—So you believe in the spirit? Do they rest, you think? So many murdered souls in the air.

—Certainly they no longer occupy the camps. I will show you, if you like. They have made Auschwitz into a piece of tourism. The East Germans come in bus loads.

—How vile, said Katie.

Alex said nothing. What could redeem such a world? He thought of the innocence of the little villages where even magnetism and electricity were a mystery; he thought of his cousins. Believers. Aron, his spine broken. Thrown by Polish Nationalists through a third-floor window in the name of pure brute virtue before the Germans came. And all the beatings and lootings, the broken glass and cut bodies. The ignorance and superstition, and the Messiah who never came.

—You know, he said conversationally : my father thought God was punishing our generation. For their lack of faith. For assimilating. Imagine that. What do the Catholics say?

—We have a Devil, said Tadeusz : I don't say it solves all the problems theologically. But at least God is no longer Commandant of Auschwitz.

—And yet my father thought God was good, mused Mendez : Men were evil, but God always good. If I could

165

only have some belief in men, I would be satisfied.

—Can't you two speak English? cried Katie, from the back seat.

To be dead, thought Lalka, here. Well, I won't be the first. And did it matter if she died? Matter? What could matter. Twenty more years. And then one way or another, blue-faced, weak, helpless. It came to the same thing. Who wanted it, twenty years swinging on a crutch? Ugly. Alone. Aching. It wasn't important.

But poor Alex. Why had she always brought out the worst in Alex? She had. She knew. Alex, be happy now. I love you. Too late. Tears came easily as she thought of him. No use. But I did love you. My way. My simple-minded way. Even if it was no use to you. My loyalty; my scatterbrained love: All sentiment. Why didn't I talk to you? When there was still time. Try and find out? No use now.

And after all. Was this the self she had defended? Against his gentle probing, his wish to enter her? How she would welcome him now, how she would call to him, it would be like an act of love. Come in, walk about in me, your questions are holy. Rare. Whoever since had asked her questions? Truly wanted her memories?

It was strange she felt no fear. Perhaps that was paralysed too. She roused herself. Yes, she had come to the point she had waited for, now she understood the absurdity of her long stubbornness. With what resolution she had defended her core from Alex. And now in Poland – of all absurd circles – she had entered it; let herself know. And there was nothing there but death. And silence.

Alex had to be directed to Lalka's bed; there so many,

and so many fearsome old faces and vacant eyes. He cried out to see her. Because he had forgotten. The softness of her skin, the solidity and roundness of her shoulders, her beauty. She was white as the pillow. Blue-white. Her lips dark purple. Her face still, eyes shut.

—Is she asleep?

The nurse shook her head.

Lalka's left eyelid opened, hearing his voice. She spoke, and the effort contorted the whole working side of her face. Alex could barely make out the words: Wait. Right in a minute. *Can* you wait? Alex.

He felt the tears start in his eyes. *Could* he wait? Her syntax hadn't changed. She was still as eager to please as a child. Afraid of being a nuisance, not wanting to disturb. Hadn't she always desired to please first and foremost? It was touching, it hurt him; and yet he remembered it was exactly *why* he had needed to get away from her; that very desire to be his creature. Disloyally he recognized how much that kind of puppetry was part of her; how hopelessly cruel he must have been to try and make her change. *Could* he wait? While she pulled herself together.

—Dear Lalka, he said awkwardly: my poor love.

He took her hand, and felt a returning pressure. Put his lips to the soft skin.

And then the voice began again, so hard to catch the words, he thought, she is saying something important. But what? About old wrongs and forgiving. She seemed to be begging forgiveness

—Don't you see? We are both wrong, he said: Answering the spirit of her tone, God, how we all waste our short lives. If only.

But if only what? He could say no more. In Polish he asked the hovering nurse: What are her chances? Tell me.

167

—The stroke was not so severe, she replied: But she has no will to live.

—Lalka, he said urgently.

And the babble of words began again; a desperate music of sadness and the sense of failure. And love; a torrent of love. He understood she was apologizing to him again. But for what he could not make out.

—I have behaved badly, always, he exclaimed: Who doesn't behave badly? As this world goes, what have we done, either of us? If you speak of what you denied me. I always understood. You did your best. It was never your fault. Never.

But clearly he was saying the wrong things. He cursed his insensitivity. Wasn't that what he had always said? Come to think of it. How could he expect that to comfort her?

At last he made out one complete phrase.

—I was no use. To you. Please. Tell me you are happy now.

—No happier.

—Please. I want to hear you are happy. Tell me you are.

Alex did not know how to answer. It was true, of course. It was a cold life he led with Lee, but then. It was not Lalka's lack of affection that had separated them. However much he might have pushed and pushed at her; it was no more love he wanted. Or loyalty. Why? Was he so perverse, so sick, that he couldn't receive simple love? As the gift it was? Probably. Instead he had searched for someone with edge and frivolity. Because it was only in such a presence he could feel himself alive. Yes, it was a sickness. How could he explain? That warm enveloping love had made him sag, made him feel old. What could he do to make that clear?

—Listen. He found himself saying, instead: You will

come back with me to Aix. When you are fit to move.

—Not possible.

—Yes, to Aix, when you are strong enough. They say you will be strong enough.

He could not read her face, but her hand trembled in his.

—You mean – after all – you *do* love me?

The simplicity of the proposition appalled him. And yet he could see in her eyes the words had meaning for her. She believed in some miracle of change.

He sighed : I always did, Lalka.

Still she shook her head. Another thought had crossed her hope. She wasn't satisfied. Suddenly he realized, with astonishment and shame, that she thought he was deceiving her. Because he expected her to die.

—Tell her, he said to the nurse urgently : tell her she will live. She must live. It's important to me.

—I'm tired, Lalka said, closing her eyes on the problem : It's a long way. We'll see, I suppose. She caught his hand. He bent to put his head on her cold white flesh.

To his surprise Tadeusz was waiting outside. Alex looked at him : I thought you were in Warsaw? But I think I understand. You were her lover, I suppose?

The younger face turned towards him, startled.

Alex tried to explain : Please, we have been strangers for many years. Don't be embarrassed, it would be absurd. Let me tell you. When she is better, I will take her back with me.

—To your mistress? Tadeusz asked crisply.

—To my house at least. Can you truly offer as much?

—She will not stay in Poland.

—Otherwise?

—There is no otherwise.

As they reached the reception desk he saw Katie was waiting patiently.

—How is she? she said at once : Tell me.

—Happier. Alex shook his head. A number of the emotions he was feeling were unfamiliar and uncomfortable. It was as though he had forgotten his own mother; and come upon her deathbed by surprise with the remorse of a lifetime neglect. For a moment he speculated with a cold eye about his adored father. Who had so long outlived his wife, and remained so lusty to the end. Perhaps he had learnt from him to admire only the strong and free; had he really been such a saintly man? As Alex had wanted to think. His strong father. His God. Had he permanently warped his son against ordinary feelings? The dream on the plane returned to him.

—I am taking her home with me, he said, however, firmly.

Katie stared at him. She looked angry, rather than pleased.

—A bloody nerve, you have. Back where? To your harlot?

—Come on. That's a silly word for you to be using.

—She deserves better.

—Look, said Mendez patiently : I want to look after her.

—How will you? Katie's voice broke in : Like an old dog? I'm not sure that's the right answer.

Alex looked at her, amused : What do you suggest? Will you take her as a gay companion to your parties?

—You know, she may well recover. Completely. What then?

With a certain brooding satisfaction, he declared, finally : Nothing you can offer will help. Don't you know that?

On their way out, the receptionist looked up and called:
Pani Mendez?

—*Tak?* Mendez approached the blonde, apple-cheeked girl: her lips were unpainted, but her eyelids were a disturbing silvery blue. For some reason her voice filled him with misgivings.

—A call for you. From the hotel.

—Thank you.

It was Tobias.

—A son? Is it strong? Mendez' voice rose for the first time since he had set foot in Poland: How is Lee?

—Lee is not absolutely well, but don't worry. The placenta came away awkwardly, so they had to give her an internal scrape. Tobias' voice was reassuring: It happens quite often I'm told. She lost some blood, that's all. The doctor is here.

—And there are no other problems?

Tobias said: Well, I'd like to know when are you coming back.

—At the moment it's impossible. I only wish I could, but Lalka isn't safe to move.

—Move to London, you mean? Do you plan to accompany her?

—I'm bringing her to Aix.

There was a pause.

—Do you want me to tell Lee that?

—Of course, said Alex, impatiently: unless I can talk to her now.

—She is pretty dopey at the moment, admitted Tobias: all the same.

—What?

—I think you should phone again and tell her yourself. Do you mind?

—It is not so easy to phone from here, said Mendez: Don't you understand? I had to make my last call from

the French Embassy. Have you any idea what it's like?
To phone Warsaw from Krakow can take four hours.
You tell her. She is not a child. Explain. A sick woman
must be looked after. Has Lacey appeared?

—Yes, said Tobias.

—Well, cope! said Mendez : Can't you?

I 2

Tobias strode up and down angrily. He scuffed at the carpet with his shoe. Mendez' arrogance was truly intolerable. *Cope*, indeed. Did he have any idea exactly what situation was developing inside his absurd fortress? Did he even understand how difficult things were already; how much Lacey had the moral ascendancy; how bizarrely it was no longer Tobias but the baby, and the baby alone, that protected Lee? In her sick room.

—I've sussed you out, she'd told Tobias: You just fancy Jack yourself, don't you? Why should I take any notice of you?

Was he really supposed to go in and see her now? Say perhaps: Very sorry, I'm told Alex is returning with his wife? Just an old friend in need. *That* would have Lacey falling about. Also it would be the signal. For whatever he was up to.

No. Tobias opened the door of his bedroom and extended the range of his night time padding. His first collapse of authority had been to read Alex' diary. How could he have succumbed to that temptation? And yet secretly, guiltily, gluttonously he had read it. Shamelessly, with Lacey's voice in his ear, looking for what? Signs of weakness, signs of *intent*? Ruthlessness? To see if Lacey was right; that underneath the gentle humane exterior was some skeletal push of avarice. Some internal voice declaring: Put money in your purse.

Well, there was nothing of that in it. Instead, a child's

voice, anguished only with the size of his father's certainties, obsessed with the chaos of them, unable to throw them off. And the journal entry:

I removed father's rings. If I sell them well, and go to North Africa, or perhaps England, not New York, perhaps I can make a beginning alone. The tickets will be easy to sell. But I can't value the rings. I shall be cheated on my first business transaction!

And presumably he was, mused Tobias: So much for Lacey's theories. If he ended up in the same bit of London as Clara and Lalka. But of course that wasn't the point. Lacey had won, simply by getting Tobias to poke about in Alex' mind. He had been corrupted, he had listened, he could no longer pretend. To stand off in rebuke.

Tobias walked about the long corridors and thought, I have lost. This is now Lacey's country. He invites his own friends. The doctor watches what is going on with more and more bewilderment. Lee locks her door.

Or does she only lock her door to me?

A cold white moon stood like a full unblinking eye in the long windows at the end of the corridor. Tobias stared into it. What a leprous, vile planet. Like the rest of the dead worlds up there. Who could believe in a God? Were the Jews demented? How could any human soul believe in anything?

His meditations were disturbed by a murmuring of voices in the well of the staircase below him. Irritated, he looked at his watch. Nearly three. Which hooligans were they? He touched his pocket; and felt the first flow of adrenalin he had experienced for weeks. For a moment he was flushed with righteous indignation. Yes, he'd go down and talk to them. Put them right. The layabouts.

Parasites. He advanced down the stairs, confident. Two turns of stairs, before he recognized the voices. And recoiled against the wall. From where he stood, he could just make out Lee, still as a frightened animal on the edge of a straight chair. And Jack Lacey at his ease, one leg cocked up, on a wicker chair that he rocked rhythmically as he spoke.

—That's all over, Lacey.

—Is it? Gone all soft, have you? Soft and bloated. I warned you. Motherhood is very enervating.

—I'm not afraid of you.

Lacey's face crackled with good humour, thin lips splitting to show white even teeth, smiling as he rocked backwards and forwards in the creaking chair.

And Tobias stood on the stairs listening. Frightened. Fascinated as an eavesdropper, Mendez' invisible watcher, creeping about. He resented it. And yet, after all, he didn't stride down and say: Stop all this. Leave her alone. Bugger off. He couldn't. Instead he stood stockstill. Listening.

—What's that?

—A bird gun. For a white, white bird. Lee, you're my prisoner.

—All right.

—Say something. If you can.

Lacey's face wrinkled with amusement at her silence.

—You can't, can you? Your spirit has rotted. There's nothing left of it any more. Why do I still bother with you, you're *dull*, Lee, *dull*.

—I don't mind.

. Lacey bent over and whispered something Tobias couldn't catch.

—Never, she said.

—You weren't averse to a little burglary once.

—That was just fun. Besides, Lee hesitated : I had a score to settle.

—Your sainted mother again.

—If you like. Those lousy snobs. They hurt and snubbed her. Because of her background. So. They're easy people to hate. It's always *good* for them.

—Don't be so sure. In some countries they'll soon be on the run.

—Poor kid yourself, Lacey. Their money's safe in a Swiss bank. They're the sort that always get away.

—Mendez got away.

—Did he? That's all you know about him. Anyway, this is my mother's house, she said queerly : Forget it. Whatever you're thinking of.

—I wasn't thinking of *lifting* anything, he said : why don't you wait and hear? If you still have any sympathies at all with the Movement?

—Are *they* the Movement? That lot out there?

—No. I'm talking about all the mothers who can't feed their babies; and all the children who haven't even got mothers. Just round the corner. Remember? In shanty towns outside Marseilles. Living in tin huts, and waiting for scraps. They could do a lot with the odd million.

—What odd million?

—Listen, he said : listen.

She listened. Their voices had dropped, Tobias waited uneasily. He thought of Mendez' words again. My mirror image. My devil. He should move. Intervene. Act. But he was paralysed. He wanted to know what Lee was going to say.

When her voice came, it was clear and angry.

—Write a letter? For money? I won't.

—Won't? Why not? He can afford it. I shan't hurt anyone if he pays up. The money isn't for me.

—I know your cause.

—You supported it once. The people are still there.

—I was playing, said Lee sullenly.

—Well, I'm not.

—Alex won't be blackmailed. Nor will I.

—Oh don't be silly, said Lacey: look at your belly and your little plump white breasts. Are you *built* to be a heroine? Don't you know I could hurt you? Smash your teeth. Scar your face.

—But you won't.

—Well, I won't have to, will I? Be sensible.

Lee put her hand to the belly, as though she still felt a child there.

—You're wrong, Jack. You've calculated badly. You *would* have to do all those things to me. I've been thinking, you see. I had no right to be happy in this house. Not here. So, O.K. Fine, you'll get what you want, Jack. But you'll have to do all the kicking and hitting first.

She spoke quite clearly and firmly.

—What's the matter with you? said Lacey: Are you joking? I don't even need your letter, if it comes to that. I only have to send a telegram, haven't I. He'll do whatever I say. And not for you either. But he wants that child. Doesn't he?

—Aren't you ashamed? she burst out: Isn't there enough blood in this earth already? The child? You'd even threaten the child? You can go to hell, Jack Lacey.

—It's my child, isn't it?

—No. *Mine*. I'm not interested in your semen. That child's mine.

Jack hit Lee hard across the face. Her lips caught on her teeth and bled.

—Don't you lecture me about women's lib. Not while half the people on earth are dying for lack of water. I tell you, the money that bloody fountain cost would save half a village.

—What do you really want? Me?

—Not now, Lacey said contemptuously: An old Jew's cast off? Or hasn't Tobias told you Alex is bringing his wife back with him?

Tobias moved on the staircase, but Lee sat still. As if stunned.

—There's someone pussyfooting about up there, muttered Lacey, peering upwards.

—I'll go away, she said: with the child. Not you. But the child. Will that do? You may as well send your telegram. What's the use? Alex will never even *know* I stood up to you.

—Oh I think he will, said Tobias. He leant over the stairs: Don't go for that potty bird gun, Lacey. I could shoot you down very much faster with this.

—Well, if it isn't the gallant Captain Ansel himself, mocked Lacey: Wonderful what a bit of pigeon-shooting will do for a man.

—National Service, actually, said Tobias: I'm quite serious.

—How long were you on the stairs?

Tobias' pale eyes hooded, but his hand remained steady.

—Long enough. I promise you wouldn't have a chance in a French court.

—For Godsake, I wasn't really going to hurt her.

—Yes, well, if you really want to stay around and

explain, I'll be happy to report my own opinion of that. Lee said woodenly: I'm going up. Let me pass.

—But you mustn't leave, cried Tobias: I promised Mendez. He'll be home tomorrow. Wait.

And then he remembered Lalka. Fatally hesitated.

—Let me by, she said: You aren't the police. I've done nothing wrong.

—For Godsake, said Tobias. He barred her way: You must be demented. Where will you go? And why? You didn't even *want* a child, remember? At first. What's changed?

—Not your business.

Lacey moved. Tobias swung round.

—Oh come on, stop playing about, said Lacey: What will you do, lock me in the library? Or the music room.

—Well no, said Tobias apologetically: I'm sorry. I'm afraid I buzzed the local police. Not a very decent thing to do, but there it is. They'll be here in a few minutes.

The bumpy roads were bad for the ambulance. Alex sat next to Lalka wrapped in her red blanket, and wondered why there were never any windows in the back; so it was impossible to see where they were going, or how far they still had to travel. Lalka was still deep in a sedative. Occasionally she moaned as the road jumped under them. It was very hot, but she clutched the blanket tightly under her chin like a protection. Or a disguise.

Alex would have liked a cigarette. He had begun to smoke again in Poland; it was almost impossible to resist the infection. But even more intensely, he wanted to arrive, to be at the château, to know what was going on. The telephone was out of order, they said at the airport. It didn't seem likely.

Lalka mumbled something he couldn't catch. But he

thought he understood. It was something about her *will;* she had drawn up her will in Krakow, leaving everything to her sister. And as an afterthought she had said, Wouldn't it be better to make it a gift *inter vivos.* Avoid death duties?

—Leave all that to Tobias, he'd said. She seemed now to be explaining her wishes to Clara.

The ambulance stopped. Lalka's eyes opened.

—Are we there? she asked.

He could see she was terrified. Afraid of Lee, he supposed, perhaps even of the château itself. But he knew the check simply meant they had changed to another route; the only safe one through the hills for a heavy vehicle.

—Nearly there, he said.

She sighed. Clutched the blanket. Closed her eyes. He too felt anxious, trying to recognize the turns in the road.

When the ambulance stopped again, Tobias opened the door.

He spoke abruptly: Lee's gone. I'm sorry.

Alex drew in his breath sharply: And the child?

—I'm sorry.

—You bungling idiot, shouted Mendez. Then he checked himself: Find someone to help.

Tobias watched numbly as the red-draped stretcher on four shoulders mounted the château steps.

—I imagine I'll be leaving too, he said: Tomorrow.

The following day, back in London, Tobias breathed diesel smoke and dead boxed air, like a tonic. He was free now, so much was clear; and he had failed. But his last job in Alex' service was a simple one, and he set about it straight away.

Clara opened the door, uncertainly, a smell of grease and eggs moving with her. Her hair was uncombed, and was now surprisingly grey at the roots.

—What do you want?

—Can't I come in?

—It's a mess.

She really didn't seem to want to open the door. Tobias said gently: I must. It's important.

—Nothing's that important. But all right come in. I can't offer you a drink.

Tobias entered and tried not to look about at a room which a burglar might have turned over. Clearly no one had washed up for a week.

—You've heard then, she said dully.

Tobias said: What?

—About Peretz.

—No. What about him? Has he left you? Tobias tried to make his voice suggest a sense of disaster.

—He's dead.

She began to cry. Big, noisy tears running down her flushed cheeks. Tobias was speechless.

—Killed himself, they say. I don't believe it. There was no need. The shop was going well. Why should he throw himself in the canal?

Tobias felt his spine prickle with horror: When was this?

—Last week. The funeral's over. Everything.

—You haven't heard from Lalka?

—Why should I hear from her?

Tobias was silent.

—Is she in Poland still?

—No.

—She's ill. That's it. Well, tell me. Don't stand there looking like the Angel Azriel.

—She *is* ill, said Tobias slowly : But recovering. At the moment she's in Aix. With her husband. I've come to bring you this. He opened his briefcase.

She took the documents and tried to focus on them : I haven't got my glasses. What are these papers ?

—For you to sign.

Patiently, Tobias explained. The documents would make her a rich woman.

She shook her head : I don't want it. Any of it.

—It's a gift.

—What will I do with it ? Now. She began to cry again.

—Clara, reasoned Tobias : get a grip on yourself. You're still young. Think of your son.

—Edward ? He left home. He didn't want to go to College. When I went to the school about it I found he'd hardly been in there all term. Peretz was right.

She began to cry again.

—What will I do with this money ?

—You could go abroad.

—Why ? What's over there ?

—You can buy clothes. Start again. Live in Lalka's old house. Look, it's yours now.

—You think I would be happy there ?

—Lalka only wants you to be happy.

—I *was* happy.

—You've forgotten.

—No, I was happy. I was some use. She never understood that, how good it feels. To be fighting for someone.

—Then use this money in some way that seems to do the same job, said Tobias irritably : Set up a trust. Be charitable.

—Money. Blood money. I don't want it.

—Whose blood ? said Tobias coldly : Are you well ?

182

—All the children. All of us. All the dead. Lalka, Mendez. All of us.

—I think you really ought to call a doctor, said Tobias : Lalka and Mendez are alive and living in Aix. Don't you understand?

A fleeting image of Mendez' great haunted head crossed his mind, but he dismissed it.

—Just sign here, he said gently.

—None of us really escaped, she said : None of us. That's all I meant.

Mendez spent the next six months in a fruitless search for Lee and the baby. Sometimes Tobias phoned, just to see how things were going; but Alex always put down the phone. The story reached the newspapers. It was hard to see how anyone as distinctive as Lee could disappear so completely against a search network that took in Latin America and Africa as well as Europe. But disappear she had.

—Stubborn. Stubborn, muttered Alex.

He had even arranged for Lacey's early release, in the hope that he might lead a trail to Lee's hiding place.

—You're off your nut, Alex, said Katie, on a rare visit : It wasn't even *your* child. We all know it. *You* know it. She was pregnant when she came. Maybe she had some screwed-up plan of foisting the kid on you at first. Maybe a hundred things. But if you want a child so much, why don't you just adopt one?

—You're so stupid, he said heavily : If you watch a child grow in the woman you sleep with, then it is your child. Isn't it?

—That's not what the doctors say.

—Don't quip. That's all it ever is, for a man. You ought to know that.

183

—Anyway, why do you want a child so much?

Alex sighed: Surprisingly – not for continuity, Katie. The opposite. To teach *someone, somehow* to be free of it all. Everything that destroyed Lalka and me. To escape.

—Well, knock up someone else, said Katie, unimpressed: or start a bloody school. You *could* say Lee escaped, she added as an afterthought.

—I could have helped her to, said Mendez: She never will now.

Alex had brought Lalka's furniture from Cheyne Walk, and given her a room facing south-east in one of the towers. She had recovered enough to sit in a chair, and look out at the olives and cypress trees, and watch the gradual success of his planting. A few vines now took the bleak white edge off the skyline.

The women who tended her hair, and clothed her each day, marvelled at her returning beauty. Her skin grew more and more pellucid. A strange contentment seemed to possess her; though she saw Alex only infrequently, and sometimes he would return to the château without telling her. Her powers of speech came and went; but whenever he did go up to see her she made sure to articulate one sentence: God has been good to me.

Alex understood that she was no longer fully in the world she overlooked; and that in some sense he was with her all the time, whether he journeyed abruptly to San Francisco to follow up some faint clue, or simply went south to the sea to pick up a girl for a weekend.

He received her blessing without discomfort; as if from a child. In a way, she had become a child. His only child. And he spoke to her always more gently than to anyone else. Sometimes, he drunkenly admitted to a stranger that, in spite of his tenderness for her, he found it deeply insulting to be needed as no more than a figure of such shadowy demands.

From the white and dusty roadside an occasional visitor would look up and catch his breath at a golden vision of her and its stillness. Sometimes, if they paused, the absolute stillness of her body made them uneasy. Catholics occasionally crossed themselves. A few legends grew up about her, but the superstitions were largely benevolent.

Alex usually looked up as he left, paused, and waved. Once, driving Katie to catch her plane, he said broodingly : I think she'll outlive us all.

—Why not? said Katie : They say peace is good for you.